I0732125

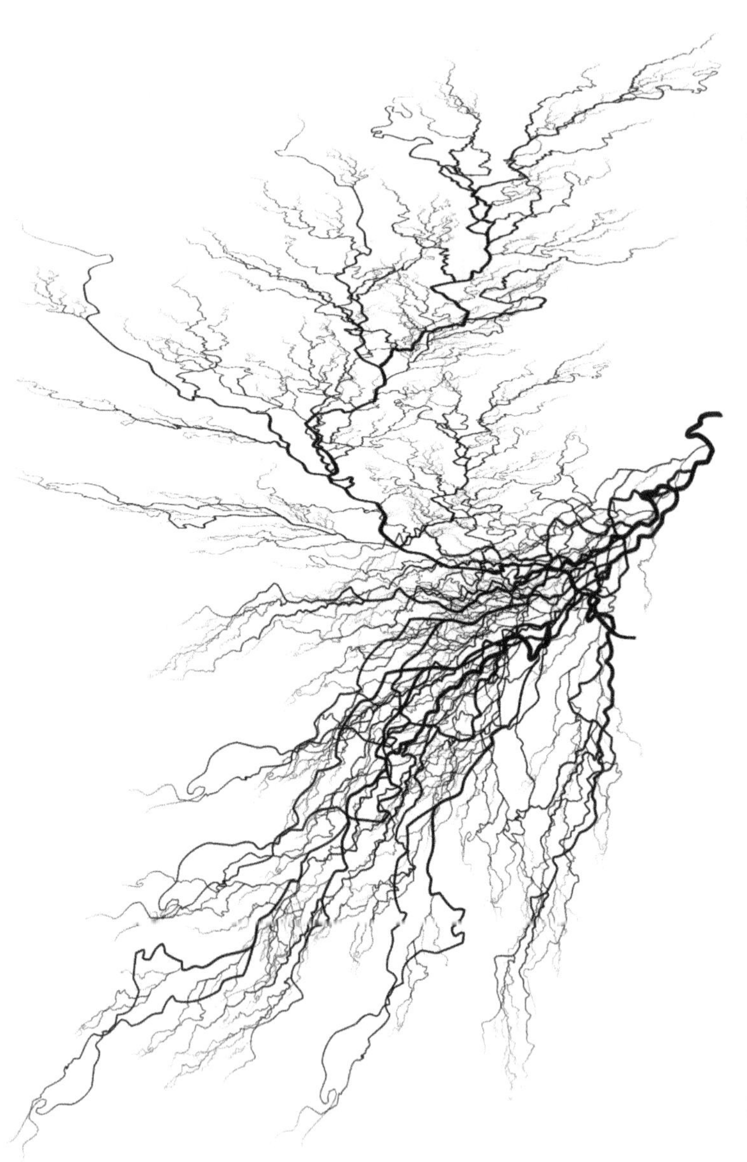

# fire starter

## covid compendium

OTHER KOKOPELLIMA PRESS BOOKS BY ANGEL BRYNNER

**Eutaxis**
**Ecclesia**
**Exodus**
**Erebus**
**Exist**
**Esthesis**
**Epicharis**
**Elision**
**Elysum**
**Empyrean**

Aolab active art  BOOK decks BY ANGEL BRYNNER

**DELUGE**
**BLOOD OF MY BLOOD**
**ZION**
**BLACKWATER**
**HALCYON**
**ZENITH**
**OVERFLOW**
**EDEN**
**FLESH OF MY FLESH**
**BONE OF MY BONE**

AOLAB Travelogues BY ANGEL BRYNNER

**BOTTOM OF THE NINTH WARD BULLETINS**
**BLACKWATER RISING**

# fire
## starter

### covid compendium

Angel Brynner

KokoPelliMa Press

Copyright © 2022 by Angel Brynner
All Rights Reserved
Printed in the United States of America by
Kokopellima Press. www.kokopellimapress.com

Library of Congress
Cataloging-in-Publication Data
Brynner, Angel
Firestarter (Covid Compendium)/ Angel Brynner
Library of  Congress control number:2020949434


Harcover ISBN: 978-1-950077-78-6
Paperback ISBN: 978-1-950077-74-8
Ebook ISBN: 978-1-950077-98-4



Cover artwork and book design by AOLAB
Additional art credits on images where needed.
Website : http://www.angelbrynner.com

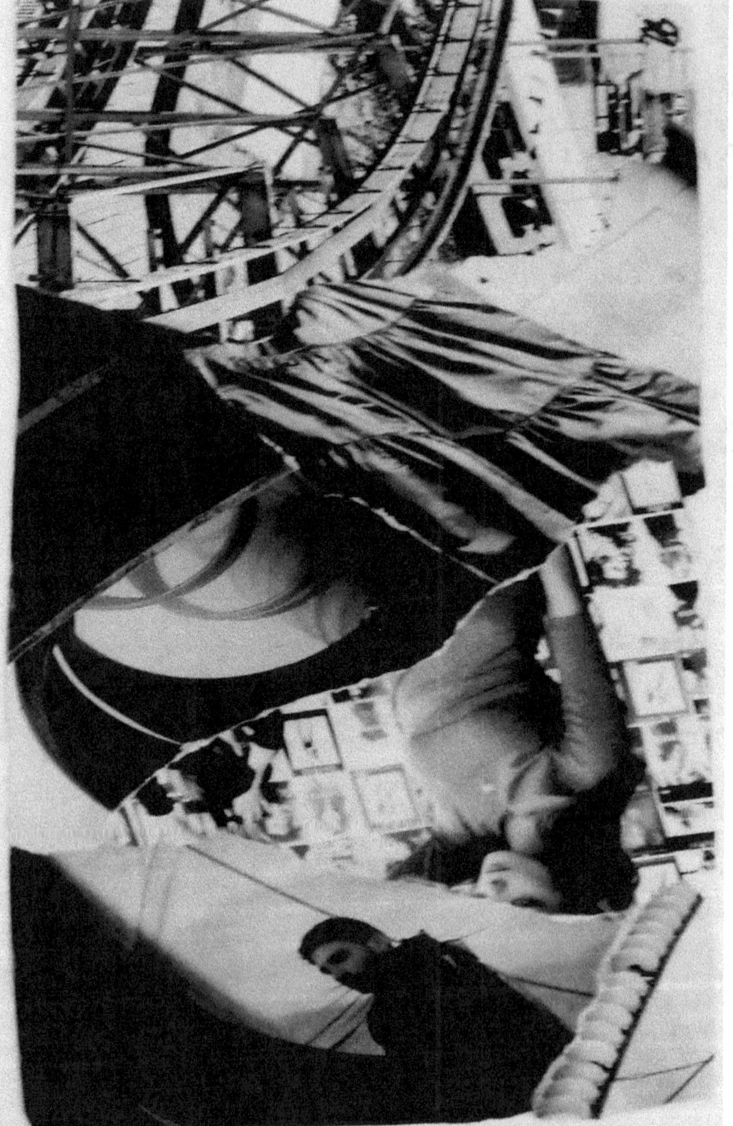

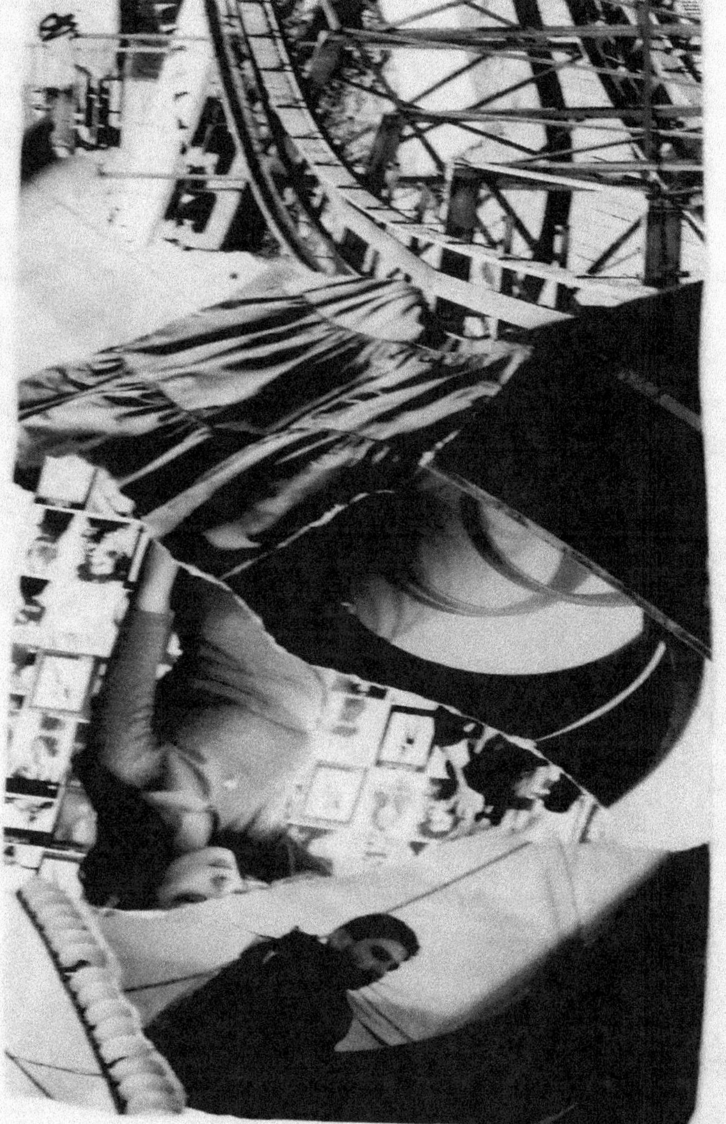

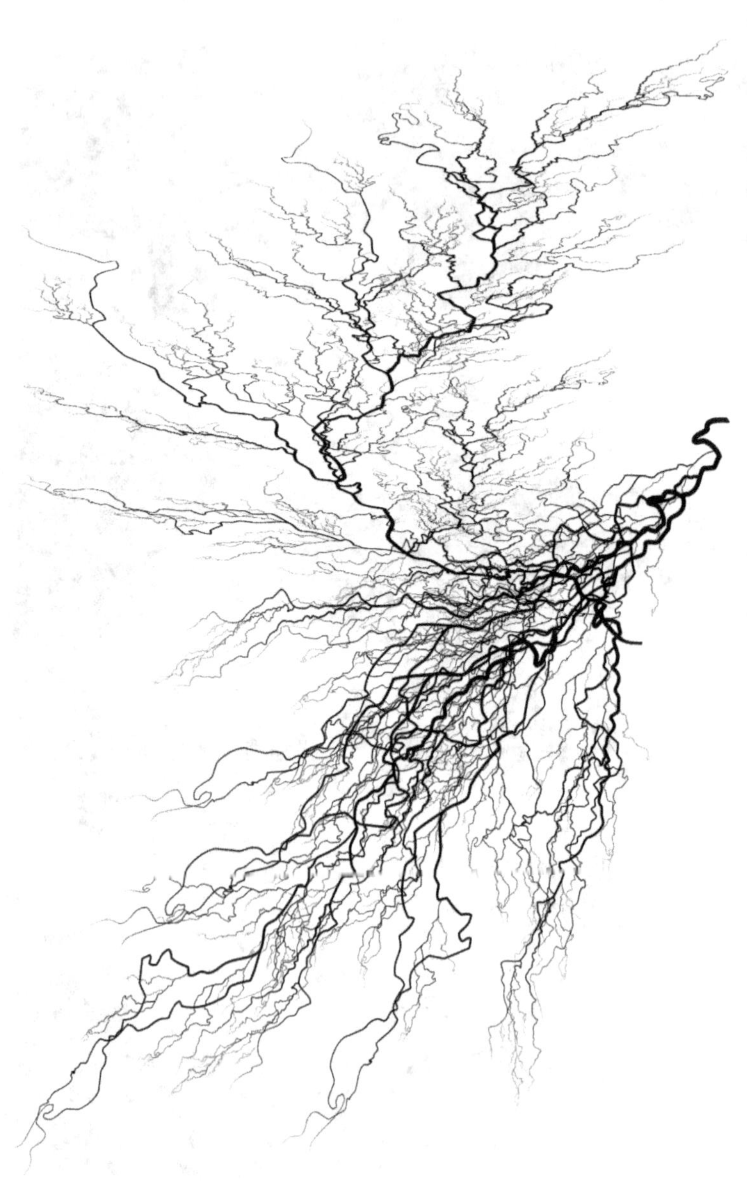

# Table of contents.

# Com·pen·di·um:

/kəmˈpendēəm/

*noun*

*A collection of concise but detailed information about a particular subject, especially in a book or other publication.*

*A collection of short-stories that came to be under the claustrophobic pressure of a 21st century quarantine, the Firestarter, Covid Compendium is the literary home-base of all the wild worlds dreamed up by author Angel Brynner outside of the /grievechronic\ universe while on lock-down due to the Covid-19 pandemic.*

*Brought to the surface of a psyche already wired for apocalyptic imaginings and isolation, each short-story is a gateway to a new realm itching to bloom into a full-fledged, twistedly beautiful standalone universe alongside Grievechronic.*

*...If we survive timelines splintering left and right.*

*Strap in, hang on...and have fun.*

**AB**

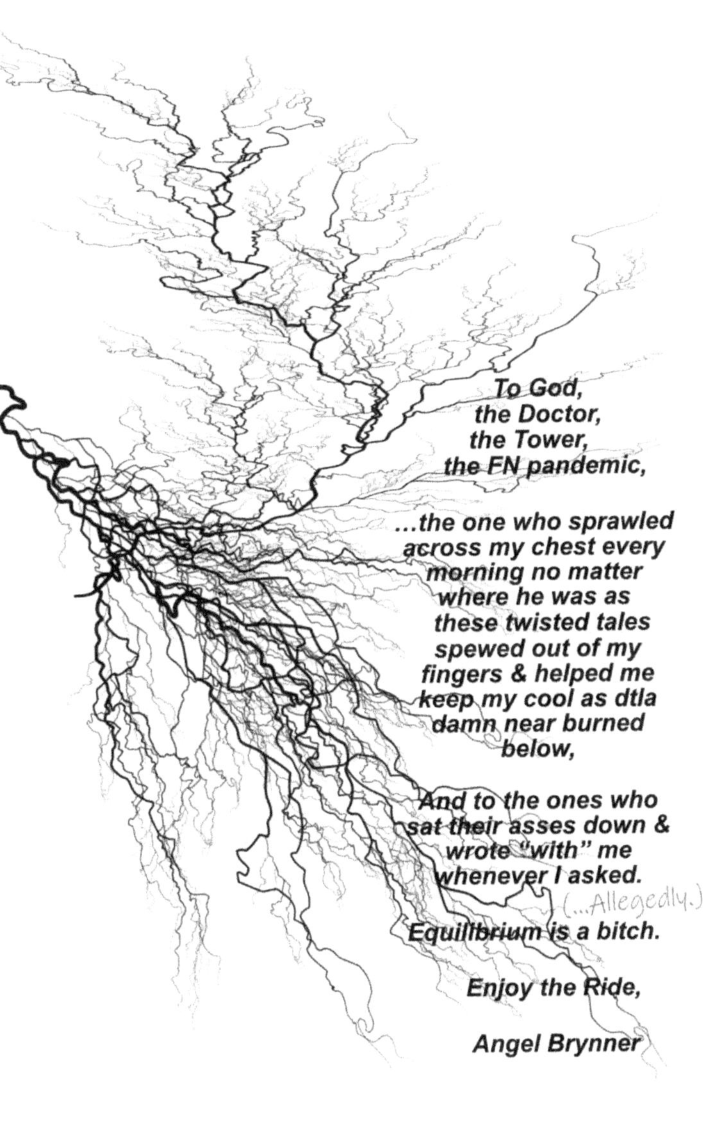

To God,
the Doctor,
the Tower,
the FN pandemic,

...the one who sprawled
across my chest every
morning no matter
where he was as
these twisted tales
spewed out of my
fingers & helped me
keep my cool as dtla
damn near burned
below,

And to the ones who
sat their asses down &
wrote "with" me
whenever I asked.
(...Allegedly.)
Equilibrium is a bitch.

Enjoy the Ride,

Angel Brynner

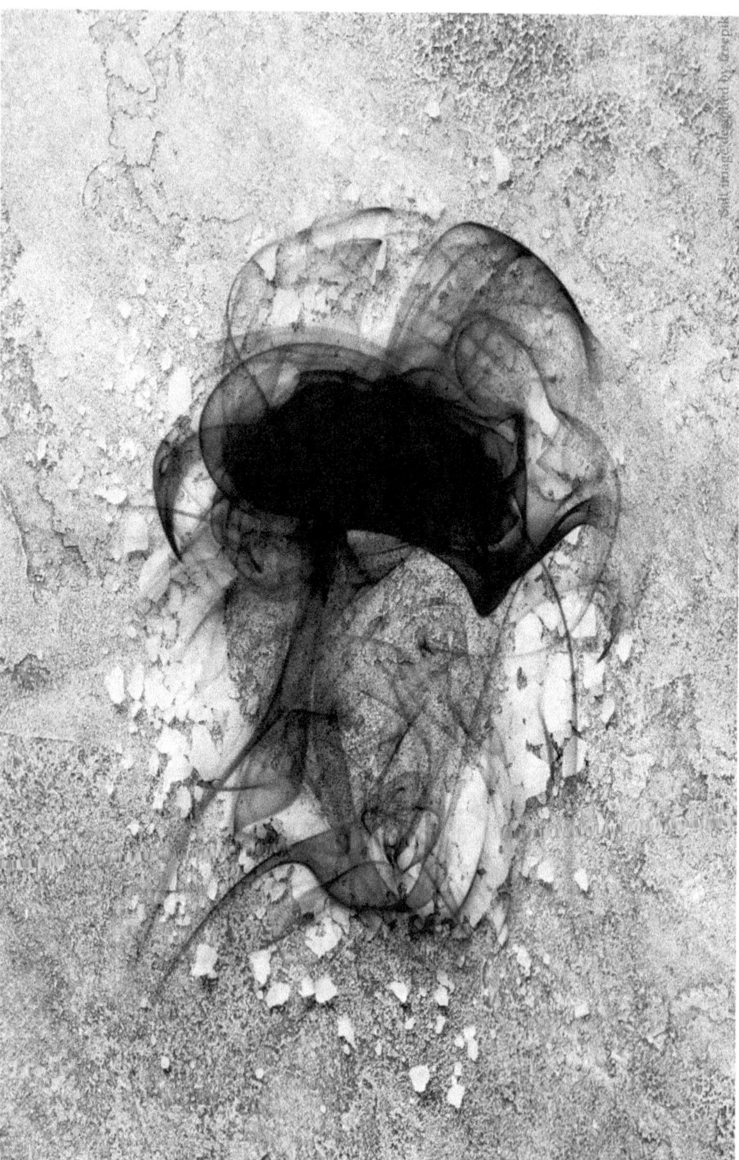

# 1.Hug.

She was transfixed as soon as they came to another one.

They'd been of no consequence the last time she was here. No need for them at all, really. But this time they were everywhere.

A warm gust of wind kicked up out of nowhere and it tried to creak to life as they both dutifully re-positioned their masks just in case.

She wondered what it'd be like to fly on them but knew better than to ask.

"No touching nada. Even for me," she said softly to herself. "Because they still can't see what this is-"

The light changed and they walked past the overturned scooter into the empty street they needed to cross. Everything shot up away from them in silence. The few other people out nodded skittishly at one another more than anything else.

They saw a few more people, this time without masks secured and looked around as they timidly pushed theirs up. The strangers waved at them in solidarity as they all stepped onto the large patch of grass that blocked out every vibratory thing wrong with anywhere else. They respectively centered themselves at far ends of the lawn and just let everything go.

Then the alarms began to blare.

The little girl and her mom hurriedly replaced their masks and headed home, the little girl looking over her shoulder to cut the eyes of those they'd just silently met into her memory in case they met again.

It hadn't happened so far.

All the eyes were different everyday out. But she still hoped like the child she was.

The alarms rung out the rest of the night. No one even knew what they were for anymore. Only that eventually they could be ignored. Like everything that had led up to this state had been.

As she drifted off to sleep she asked her mom what to call them again.

"Wheels, baby. Wheels on a kick scooter, " her mother murmured and kissed her forgetful daughter on the forehead before turning off the lights and going to rest herself.

The closet door creaked open.

"How was it?"she whispered.

"It was great! Wait til you see the Wheels!"the little girl trilled softly.

"Yeah, they have those in my last one too, just underground-" she laughed. "Wheels are cool. See you tomorrow?"

"See you tomorrow-" the lil girl crawled out of bed to make way for her self from another timeline and went to the bedroom door.

"What are you-" she asked from the bed.

"I...just wanna kiss her goodbye...she's a really nice one-" she whispered. "They aren't always. I like her hugs."

"Okay, just don't fall asleep. Remember what happened last time," she said with authority.

"I know, I know-" she giggled and tiptoed down the hall. Her mother was on the couch in the dark. The muted TV tossed shadows up against the white walls.

"Bathroom?" her mother asked. She nodded, lying to her, then crawled up on the leather couch and hugged her.

"You're a good momma-" she muttered in her arms.

"& You're a good kid," her mom murmured back, kissing her forehead again.

"I hope I remember this," the little girl whispered.

"You will. There's a lot going on. We're all forgetting everything. Think that's part of their plan. But don't worry, I'll be here to remind you. For Now...go on back to bed."

The little girl nodded, hugged her mother one last time, went to her room, entered the closet and disappeared.

...To be continued.

Elsewhere.(C) 2020 AngelBrynner.

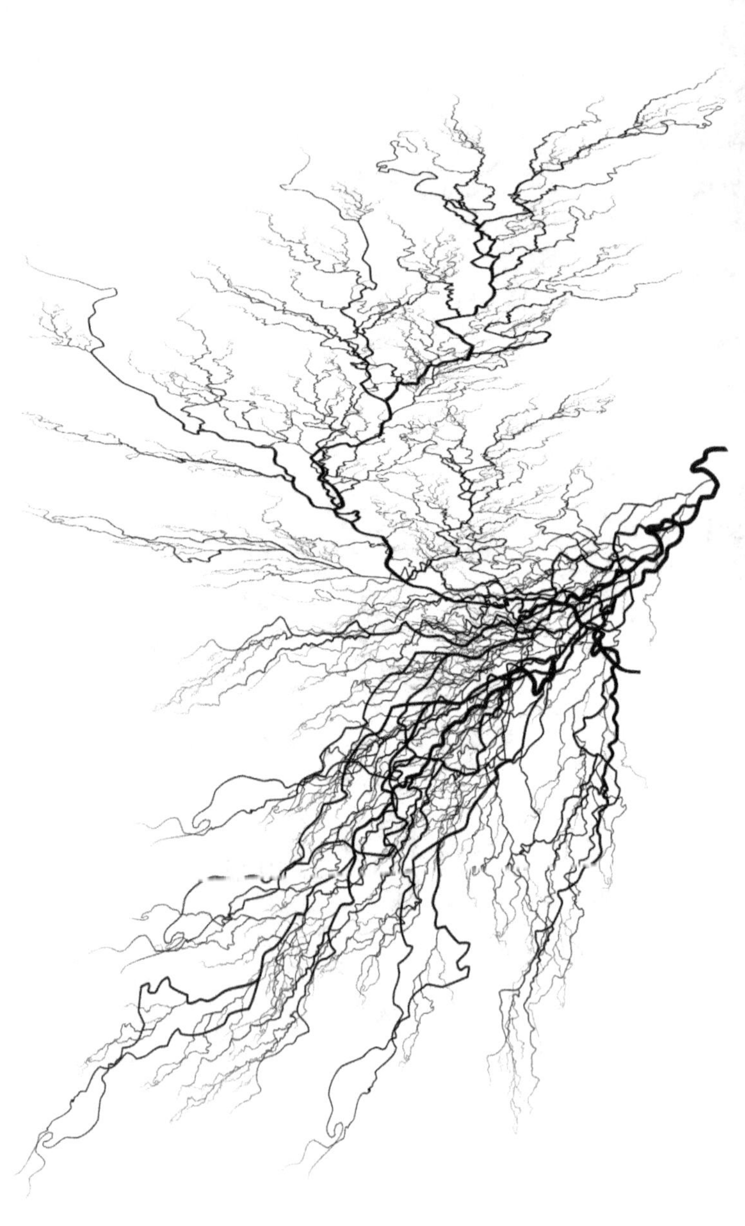

# 2. Alset

She walked through the neighborhood one last time.

All glass that could be boarded up on ground floors was.

Had been since days before Samhain.

The wind whistled through the few trees left standing.

Massive cut downs under the guise of staving off a

potential aerosolized wave that could use the final

pollination of the region in its favor.

Algorithms sent thousands with specific sensitivities to

Russian thistle into localized panics that generalized and

caught fire in the media as an overall allergic invasion "on the way" that went viral, an elegant 'controlled burn' of the highest order.

By the harvest moon regions that had been triggered into demanding to be deforested at breakneck speed breathed nervous sighs of relief and tried not to be put on edge by the absence of the sound of birds they'd been accustomed to hearing since birth.

By the Blue moon the work that the AI services had been procured to make room for was done.

Barely anyone had noticed the newly deemed essential workers constructing stout, strangely cumbersome cell towers at a fever pitch in communities behind the fearful frenzy that had been kicked up.

But she did.

The rushed 5G construction had danced quietly with the repaving and polishing of streets for their big moments in the absence of traffic due to almost everyone hiding in their homes until cloaked pregaming bells were rung signaling it was time to skirmish. It was like clockwork, the killings and the protests that erupted on their heels afterwards as tests, a precision that got tighter and more menacing the closer the world marched towards decision day.

She'd watched the world gearing up to get caught in the teeth of its own despotic machinery mostly with peace. Because there always had been a point to the escalation in the past, an inexplicable peace keyed into being given the wherewithal to see it all from the underside of the machine, spat out of it without having to be a cog.

She had strange faith the proverbial providence in all of this building up was for it to be knocked down once and for all and she stuck to it, even when it made her look stupid.

She visited the water one last time.

The atmosphere around it still burned her eyes, justifying the caution tape that had been strung around it sans explanation.

Joggers who'd set their courses by continually crossing paths with her pensive pace slowed down and smiled with relief at seeing her after her absence. They nodded at each other and went on their way a little lighter. The runners had thought she'd succumbed.

She had, but in a way she wouldn't be able to easily explain. She'd surrendered to it. All. & embraced the gifts the outer insanity had given her. Believing for next nows, whatever those holy nows meant themselves to be.

She looked up at the silvery clouds with resignation and the cornflower blue sky above them with hope, then went home to wash the smell of outside off her skin and out of her hair.

*

The engineering quarters of the telecommunications companies were solemn.

Their loved ones had been relocated out of the test areas to safety, which should have been enough according to what they had thought they'd believed before they'd gone through with betraying humanity.

They made their way down the hallway that emptied into the viewing center.

"Figure out a man's frequency & you can shatter them as you see fit" marched in block letters down one wall, "If you want to find the secrets of the universe, you must think in terms of frequency and vibration" down the other. Tesla's name was falsely attributed to both quotes, totally getting the heart at the center of Tesla's work backwards.

No one could look each other in the eye.
Because it was time.
The burning was about to begin.


*

Completely shorn, when she climbed out of the scalding water the advertisements for 5G going live rung out in celebration above every empty corner & wired for 5G smartphone and console in the region simultaneously.

...A moment later the clashes began to break out.

*

Everywhere. People blindly flooded into the streets, swinging.

They went wild as they looked for those to attack for trying to push towards change. Their vibrational depravity was broadcast around the world to stoke more fear, the latest launch of an perversely addictive, insidious version of reality TV, live in a sick, bloodied instant.

In hopes of ensuring those that the monsters in power needed to stay out of it all would.

...Like clock-work.

But there was a caveat.

One that neither the AI, the engineers nor those who signed their checks had counted on.


...Those they'd programmed the decimating hordes to target in the streets had already handled their business. They had no reason to pay mind to bells struck that the powers that be had not bothered figuring out how to un-ring as all hell broke loose. They were all at home and mostly offline. Because the word had spread.

"Turn back your clocks and off your 5G capabilities at midnight. "


The decimators decimated themselves in the absence of the targets they'd sloppily been programmed to hit ....

and would not stop until they'd fully cannibalized

themselves in the streets for the entire world to witness in

awe.


& it'd All be thanks to 5G.

*

She opened the windows and stood airdrying her raw skin

as screams echoed below from the east & west.


She'd seen the stationary ad announcement on the

inspirational channel she had playing in the background

on the computer she kept precisely due to its inability to

register any G above two.

Naked except from a mesh thong, wet hair dripping down

her back, she settled down onto the floor. Water

protectively pooled around her as high noon hit and she

fell into prayer.

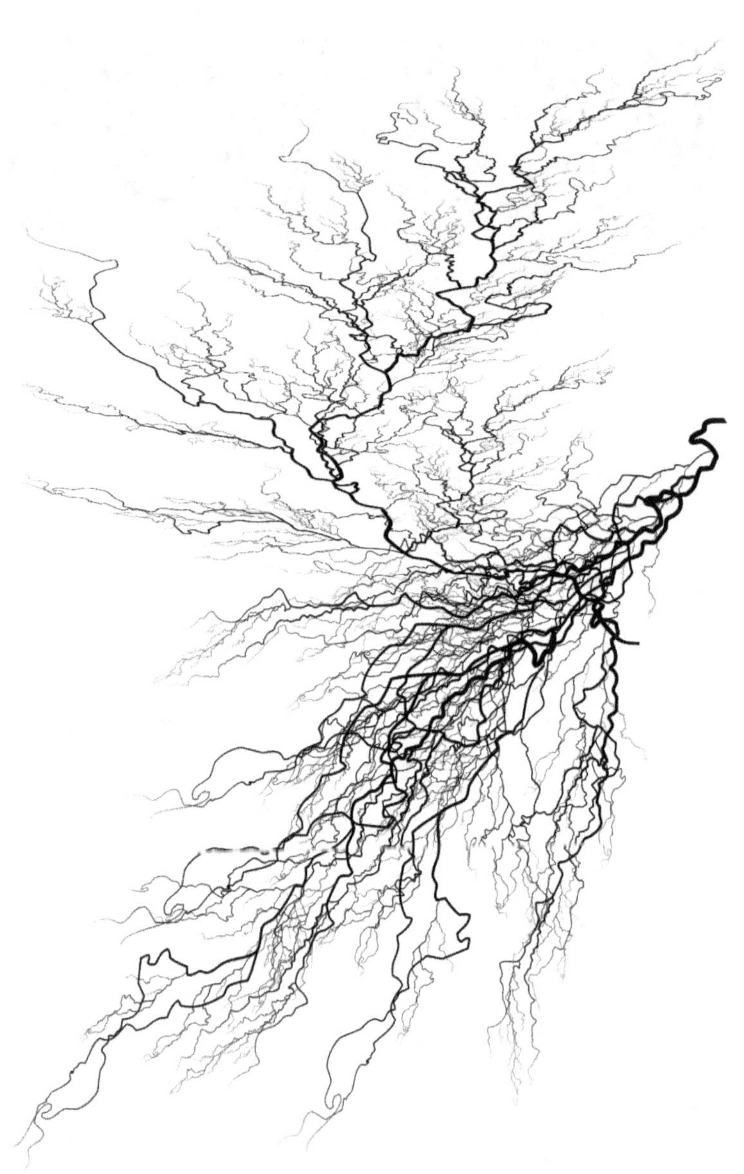

# 3. Savior

"We've got to get him to understand this-"

He looked over his shoulder at the door they huddled on the other side of. "Under the circumstances do you really even think that is possible anymore in lieu of-?"

The color drained from his face. "We have to try or the entire thing is-"

"Gentlemen, they're almost ready for you now-"

Their heads popped up in shamed shock that they shook off to remain viable.They adjusted themselves, looked at one another and streamed across the threshold, following the disembodied voice.

They entered the window lined hallway that looked out on two seas of people separated by soundproofed mirrors that lined the walls of both waiting rooms and gave no hint of the proximity of one angrily huddled mass to the other.

The first sea of protesters threw projectiles and placards at the fissured glass surface that was all that stood between the two men and their textbook mayhem.

The epitome of entitlement and compulsive composure, he arrogantly jutted out his chin as his eyes slithered across the crowd, rueing their existence and the fresh air they didn't deserve that was piped in as some pseudo-semblance of due process in troubled times.

Ropey veins sprawled across his face like a sploom of spit out of the collar of his $1500 starched shirt tucked into a pauper in these parts $2500 suit. They pulsed and snaked across his temple as thoughts of derision and disdain for the masses carved themselves into his splotchy, translucent skin.

He jumped like the coward he truly was as an angry body in the fray slammed into the hallway window. The masked protester glared as if he could see him through the looking glass and spit. The lougie mimicked the splay of veins too perfectly across the surface of the glass to be ignored. He shuddered.

His partner stifled a chuckle. "Should we have that removed?"

He glowered, trying to save face. "Use the moles to move

It towards the door. Turn up the heat. Let it out at the last

so it can-"

His partner shook his head and smirked, whispering into

the piece as his partner stormed down into the second half

of the hall.

Wordlessly, the protester was surrounded by brethren

who banged roughly on the windows around him,

wedging btwn him and it until he was pushed down the

line and back into the outskirts of the heated crowd.

After watching for a few beats his partner picked up the

pace around the bend and crashed into him staring in

disbelief into the huddled masses of the second sea.

Memorabilia coated believers were garishly smushed into their holding pen, waiting solemnly for the slightest nod of healing from their invincible savior. They'd made their way in shellshocked droves, quietly admitted at all hours of the night to wait for audience in the ventilated space.

The weaker they became the more they hallucinated they'd been transported to a broad plain, a room without windows or walls full of a neverending ocean of faithful just like them. They ghoulishly swayed back and forth in clusters under the loop of last time's benediction that played across scrims embedded into the ceiling of the space at intervals to literally keep their heads up so as not to mind the bodily waste and heaving clumps of humanity that crawled around closer to the floor.

"Come on," he muttered to his partner who stood there entranced by the garishness of the believers covering up their coughing and wheezing by thunderous outbursts of applause known to placate their guy. The heartbreaking attempts at rolling rallying cries were what snapped him out of it enough for them to continue on their way.

They reached their destination and the door was swung open just as the roar of the waiting crowd spun from feverish to frantic.

He looked over towards the sound and by default them before she could discreetly extricate herself from between his knees. She stood up and pressed the wrinkles in her skirt down her thighs with one hand as she dragged a perfectly manicured thumb around the outskirts of the lush oval of her mouth, exiting the office.

"Gentlemen," she growled throatily as they both averted their eyes while she passed.

"Sir, um-"

"Listen to it, isn't it grand?!" The savior sung out, as rhapsodic over what had just been relieved as he was to the cheers that were obviously full of excruciating pain to all others present.

"Sir, they're dying. In numbers that are overloading the burners below-"

"Then send them home-"

"They won't make it, Sir-"

"Who needs them to make it?"

"Sir, the ones that can-they'll riot if we try to disperse them without seeing you-hearing something from- And.. they're hungry...Sir-"

He sighed at the inconvenience. An armed guard suggested a run through of the newest material on his desk.

"Ah~ yes! The new speech-writer's delivery! Excellent!" He smiled repugnantly."You know that kid really knows her way around a pen-"

"You should be very proud, Sir-"

"Sir, is it okay if I-" his partner began.

"Wanna watch? SURE! COME-"

"Excused- if I am excused."

A tremor of insecurity bloomed across the savior's face as it twisted up in outrage that he swallowed. "Fine." He said flatly.

"Just-just a bathroom break, Sir-" his partner whispered nervously.

"FINE. Fine. FINE!" He snarled. "Catch up with us quickly after you've relieved your self-"


His partner scurried off as they parted ways and headed down opposite directions of the hall. He flinched as he heard the whizz of the silencer behind him, then the echo of his partner's bones crunching to the ground in the sack of dead flesh he'd volunteered to become. He leaned against the outside wall as the savior went in, a solitary tear sliding down the side of his face that he didn't wipe away as his hand tensed on the butt of his glock.


The Savior entered the protective pope-like bubble to greet his greatest fans, oblivious to the oblivion around him. He whipped them into a rambunctious frenzy.

"It is as if your mortal enemy was closer than you could possibly imagine..." he sung out over the rapt crowd as the vents on their side were opened. "And what kind of Savior would I be if I didn't offer you the...Option ...of...a Blaze of glory-?"

On the other side of the mirrored wall protesters screamed out against the heat. A few were allowed to leave. The spitter was the last one maneuvered through the doors.

Drenched in sweat, he heard his comrades cheering for the A/c kicking on and the strange, exaggerated sound of vents opening before the harsh clanging of bolts being locked from the inside and out by those classified as expendables.

He nervously picked up his pace as the color fled from his face.

"And I'm a Great Savior! Aren't I?! AREN'T I?!" his voiced roared down from speakers strung overhead as he tried not to run. "I PROVIDE MANNA AND MEAT FOR my Tribe!! Eat and be full!!" Savior screamed maniacally.

The gift that had let him see where to spit crashed him to his knees as bullets began to silently slice through the air around him, making it seem like he was hit. The marksman whispered into his piece without even bothering to go out and check the body.

"DONE." He muttered and walked away.

The masked protester laid on the ground, eyes ripped open in shock as he saw in his mind's eye the mirrored walls separating.

The seas pivoted, exposing the embittered protesters to the wretched, whipped up, infected and famished dregs of society that made up the corps of true believers in the Savior's camp.


"Food!" A wasted away follower screeched. Others followed suit.
"FOOOD!!"


"What the hell?!" A protester yelled, alarmed.
The haggard followers of Savior lurched towards the aghast protesters as the sickness that had hung thickly in the air around the former slammed through the A/c vents onto the latter, an assault above and in front of them.

"HEY! They've locked the doors!" someone screamed. "They've locked the fucking-"

The very real screams from the protesters being cannibalized as Savior jumped up and down gleefully in his protective bubble from the speakers overhead snapped the Masked one back online.

Shaken, he crawled into the bushes and frantically pushed his way through a quarter acre of trees. He came out on the outskirts of a separate, unknown entry pavilion leading back up to the space and whipped off his windbreaker in a panick as the speakers on this side screeched patriotic songs over the heads of the weary, emblazoned faithful on pilgrimage to see their Savior.

He backed away until he felt safe enough to run and took off.

Savior looked out over the traumatized remnant of protesters and ordered the doors to be unlocked. They struggled out of hiding places and ran for their lives as the cleaners moved in.

They wouldn't be believed and would have infected entire encampments before they dropped dead. Just like every group of social justice warriors with the audacity to stand against his regime had done across millennia.

Fat off the kill, the viral disease riding his reptilian brain didn't notice all the bloodied bodies of his guards on the floor until it was too late.

He wrathfully unscrewed the silencer as Savior looked at him in shock.

"Pow!powPOW!"

He shot him in the head-the seat of the infection's power, in the lungs-for all those who'd lost their lives in this invasion, and in the groin for what had become of the speechwriter.

With hollow point bullets.

Disgusted, he kicked what was still left intact as Savior's body over onto its stomach and emptied his clip, screaming.

"AND THIS IS FOR EVERY FUCKING PARTNER OF MINE YOU FUCKING KILLED during this shit, YOU SICK SONAFA BITCH! I Should've killed you eons ago, you sick Fuck!!"

He sobbed like a child and slumped down the nearby wall onto the floor as he lost his mind, covered in splatters of Savior's blood and hunks of his flesh, heaving as the hall itself seemed to tilt and waves of Savior's blood crashed towards and over him as he blacked out.

When he came to, he and Savior's corpse were surrounded by a half circle of perfectly polished black shoes.

One cautiously leaned down as the others loomed overhead.

"Sir, Sir- we saw it all- are you alright?" he said. "We," he motioned towards the other suits,"saw it all- are you okay?"

He watched as another bent down and roughly cut what remained of his face off of Savior.

"That should fit just enough, crown-wise-" the cutter grinned malevolently.

He deftly pulled the gun strapped to his ankle out and shot all of them in the knees, then heads as they fell. He grabbed the skinned face of Savior, those who could make the call to stop him dead in the hall alongside their illustrious leader.

He ran out of the crowds streaming into the complex through the front door into the night.

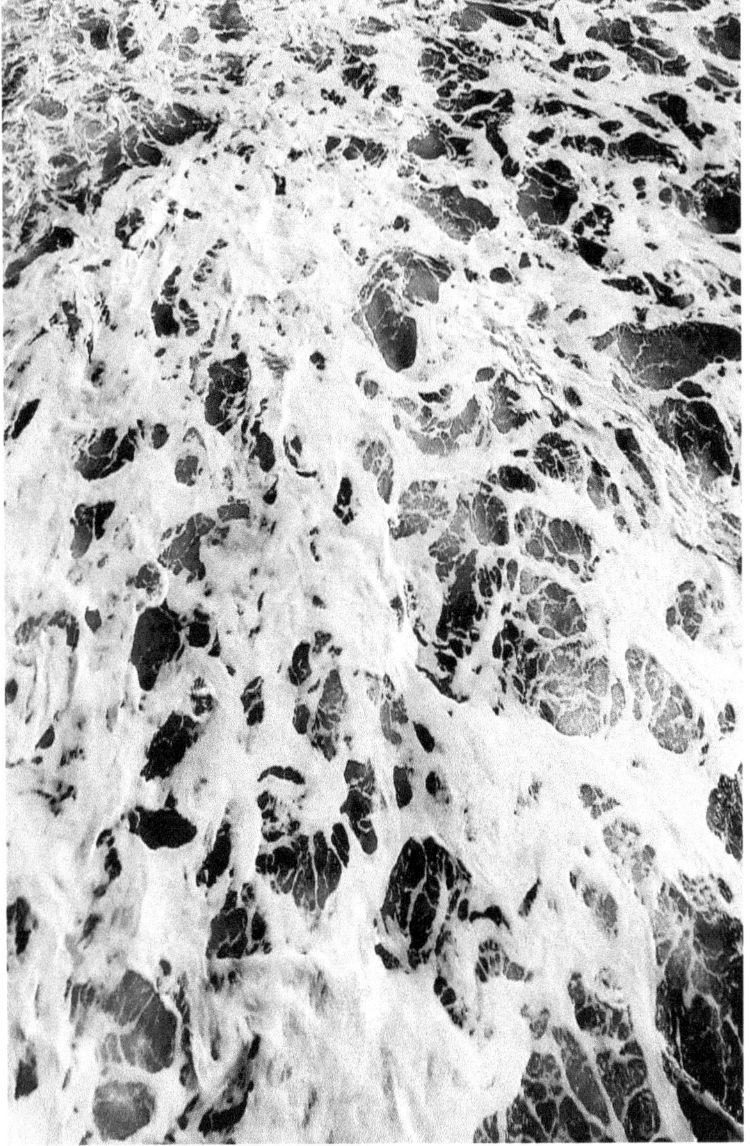

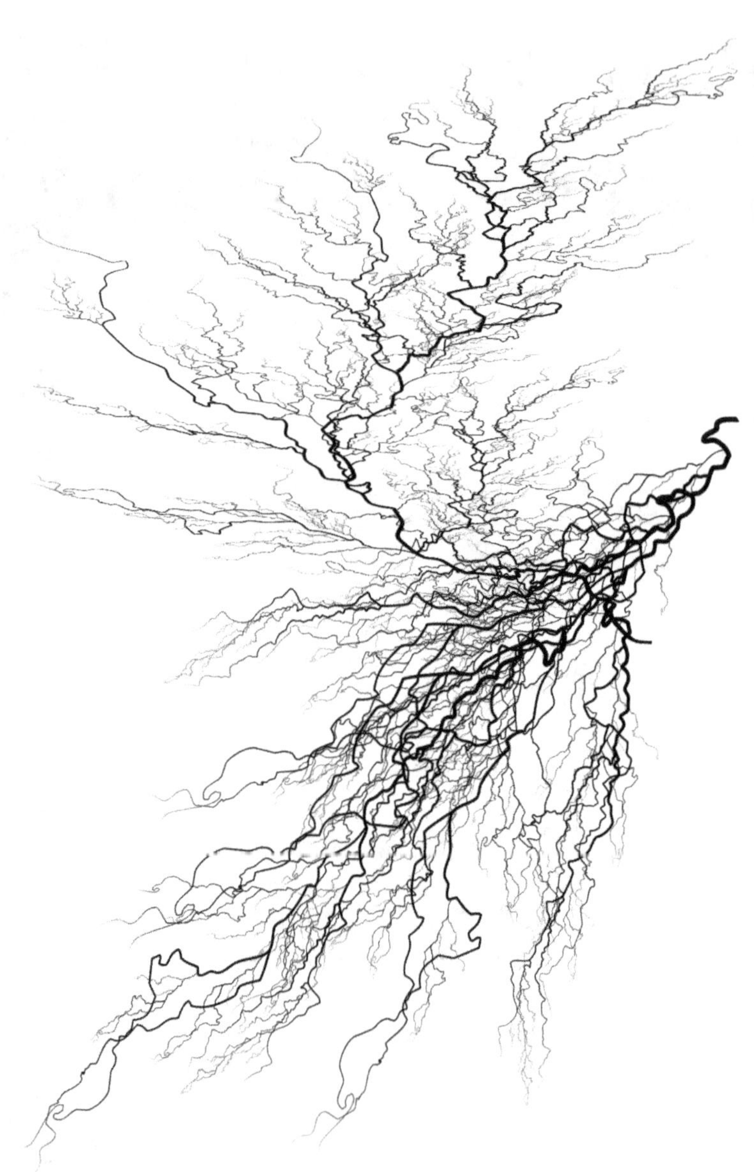

# 4.oasis

They warily looked around.

The half-light made it just possible to see the branches pulse overhead as more thick condensation dripped towards them in slow motion.

The slow throb of the drum in the distance made them feel underwater but they weren't and knew it because their training had kicked in immediately when they'd come to. But what they hadn't been prepared for was what echoed through the silence at jagged intervals they could attach no rhyme or reason to.

High-pitched wails pressed across the dank, confining landscape they'd awakened in, as if a ruined temple somehow still stood in the rubble of their earlier waves over hills and valleys they could not see in the dark. Faith where there was supposed to be none, according to all drills.

"There's nothing that can be done with that-" they muttered, keeping to themselves as the rest woke out of stasis and surveyed things seen through the already awakened one's eyes.

Faith was not the feast they were there for. It was fear that was the bounty, longed for like breath to a drowning man.

Fear was the harvest.

Fear was the plumb line they'd desperately craved and landed in droves for. And they only had a fortnight to follow it to fruition. For the sake of kingdom come. Before they died off like princes, cast into fiery reaches they'd been promised dominion over, crowned heads first.

This realm was reported as a most fickle one pedagogically, yet they all knew the intel was solely theoretical the moment they'd been roused by the incessant, almost defiant drumming in the distance.

"This invasion will be a success," they muttered to themselves, on mission.

"Find the fear... and do it anyway, " they groused in unison as they pressed forward in search of the storied seat of it in the dark.

The squadrons made short work of the cells they'd awakened capsized and captive in, leaving nothing but carnage in their wake as compatriots splashed down from the branches behind them.

But the faith in the atmosphere mutated the encasement nerves protectively coursing across the surfaces of them. Made them minutely malfunction before they knew what was happening.

Overhead, indecipherable invocations frantically screeched from the ruined temple beyond the basecamp's horizon-line, seemingly getting louder in response to the movements of the squads.

It was fear.

"... Had to be," they assured each other in the dark.

The influx emboldened them, made them regroup, turn

what read as due south, prepare to charge forward.

All but one and the misfits that followed them.

The one who'd been upbraided when it had been disclosed

that they'd taken the time to discern the linguistic patterns

in place where they were being sent into.

"They're belligerent animals, no further 'understanding' is

necessary!" their superiors had railed. They'd gone so far

as to have threatened them with the equivalent of a court-

martial on the other side of the mission if they'd heard one

more reference to it.

Still something made them stop, tilt their astutely

crowned head to the side in the heavy atmosphere, in

understanding, holding their ground as the others charged forth.

The other misfits followed their example as everything else around them sped into action.

The feverish screams spiraled up as soon as the first of their infantry tripped the line.

They froze as it dawned on them all at once that they'd thrown themselves out into the open. Their own stores of fear got tapped as danger became very real to them for the first time in the hostile environment they'd mistaken as passive. They'd landed with barely enough to reach the fabled Låñerđæ oasis and load up, and depleted their interim reserves almost immediately. Collectively they panicked.

Suddenly, the land itself seized up so violently that the slaughterhouse cells changed directions en masse and slammed into each other, mistakenly brutalizing one another while trying to protect themselves in the dark.

It got quiet above the carnage and chaos of their own creation. No chanting, no drumming, no motion in the branches behind them. Only the slow, pained moans of their own.

As the stock-stilllmisfits watched from behind, faint whiffs of the fear they'd entered the ecosystem to feed on danced across their comrades sensors and soaked through their suits. It licked their faces lasciviously, until they were drunk off of it, unable to discern if the terror seeped from them or they were surrounded in fear native to the hostile plain.

Then the rains began.

The misfits ran in reverse, taking cover from what pelted their crowned suits like volleys of fire as their brethren were decimated on the field the upstart who'd comprehended the gist of the word prayer had refused to step out on.

Their platoon blindly ran backwards until their legs gave out, slamming through a crevice and roughly down an abyss slick with what had the stench of bile and coated them like mucus upon entry, causing them to black out.

They came to on the shores of the Låñerðæ oasis.

"Oh my- Are you kidding me?!" one of them gasped.
"They were headed the wrong way the entire time-"

another whispered as they all bowed belly to ground in front of the fabled seat of faced fears they'd been sent into this ecosystem to feast on.

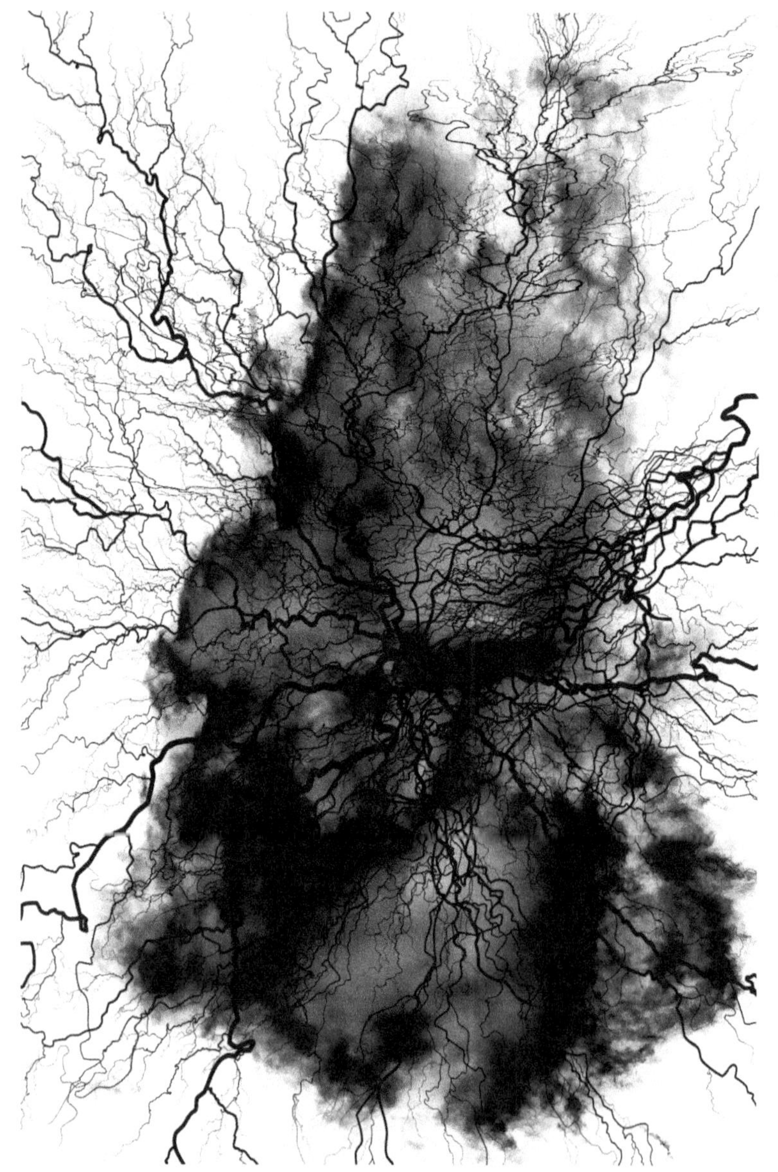

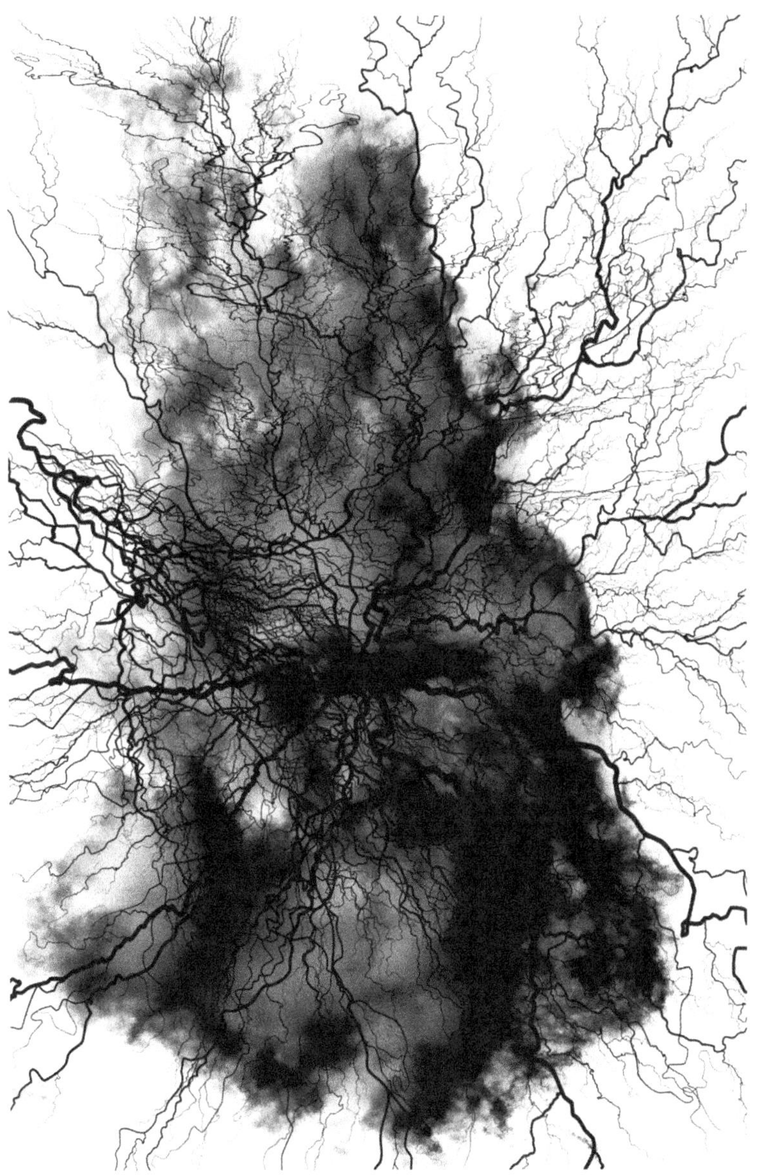

# 5. Nymph

She woke up with a gasp, choking on it.

Felt the stickiness surrounding her

The way she always did as everything started to

disintegrate.

The dankness hung heavy around her, closer than anything should have ever been allowed to be.

Everything she'd finally purged lay beside her, in ruins. She was worn out by its proximity, from the caginess inherent in being beside something inert that had once consumed so much from the inside.

The truth rammed itself up her nose like a rod of light.

She'd die in here alongside it if she didn't escape this night. She started to claw, up and out the only directions she still had enough comprehension of to pursue.

She screamed against the sensation of her vocal cords dissolving, her fingernails flaking off into wet dust. The back of her head was as repulsively moist as whatever she rammed into. The corpse of what she'd carried within, what she'd stopped shy of turning into, leered at her as her eyes collapsed into the pile of goo she was without it. But her spirit screamed on, soundless.

Her heart scratched through unseen surfaces like the absence of hands meant nothing in light of its intent. Until suddenly everything went silent.

An agile fingered palm rammed through the chrysalis as they all watched, enthralled. Those with no reserve cheered enthusiastically as they watched her climb out in awe of what she'd become.

The lead stepped forward as she steadied herself on the other side, erect in the muck of before. He smiled, leaned in, whispered darkly.

"Now just what...are you ...supposed to be?"he slurred almost erotically.

She tilted her head, bemused he didn't know. "You'll see,"she murmured back. "Now rinse this shit off of me."she ordered.

He stepped back, reminded of his place in this, and nodded dutifully. So the veneration could begin.

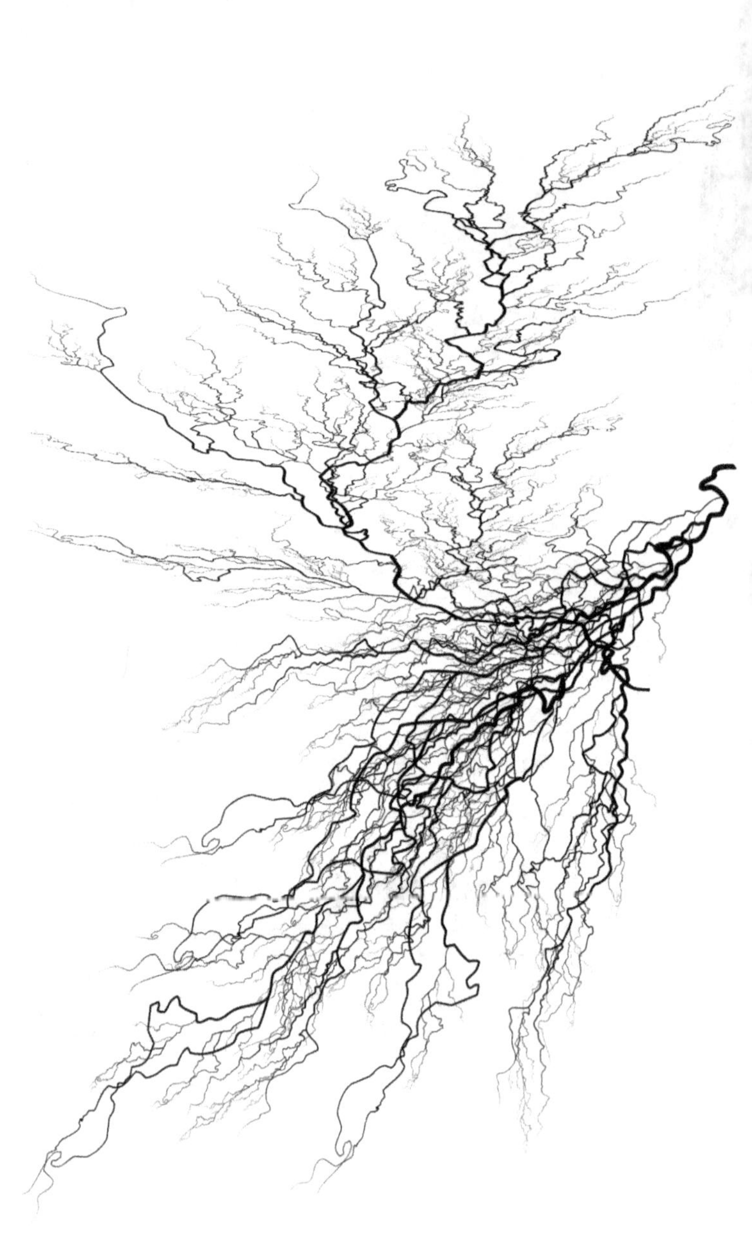

# 6. Palm

"4:54..." she muttered to herself without looking up from her notes.

It was 458pm.

She re-transcribed quotes and paragraphs she'd scrawled on scraps of paper on the road into their stiff, new storehouse. They'd stay there until it was time.

The sun flooded into the room she was folded up on the floor of, making it stuffy. Beams of light bounced off of mirrored walls and cast rainbows across her skin and the mountain of balled up scraps of her already reworked words behind her.

"459-" she muttered.

It was 7 o'clock. She hadn't left the space in days, let alone noticed the sun go down hours ago.

There wasn't even a memory of turning on the lights on the far side of the living room in her mind's eye, let alone of having scooted almost completely under the table in the place as she worked, protectively, like a child dreaming.

"There," she said, content.
She looked all the way up and stared at the space around her in the mirror.
She tilted her head to the side. The reversed tiny handprint caught the light as it always did.
"Almost done, " she whispered.

Her heart shook so hard that her body didn't recognize the

4.3 earthquake making

the tower she was trapped in sway.

She was calmed by the space filling with the sound of

laughter that used to erupt out of her as a kid in

celebration of some gargantuan at the time task, whether

anybody else cared or not.

The tremor passed.

She crawled from under the table, stoically picked up each

balled up piece of paper and gently lobbed them into a

straight line up against the mirror before turning out the

light and shuffling off to bed.

*

She woke up roughly.

The entire apartment smelled of the sanka her dad used to let her drink as a kid to the chagrin of her mother, never telling her until she was 17 that it was decaffeinated. She smiled to herself.

As soon as her feet hit the floor the sirens started again. Maybe they hadn't stopped. They were just another layer of sensory trauma now, noise to be ignored like another channel she hadn't figured how to turn off.

She walked into the living room and looked outside. Clouds of carrion dove into the rubble that spread out where the rest of the city used to be like seagulls on the shore, picking up who knew what, fighting over it in the air.

Glass that had been crushed by repeated blows to

reflective sand shimmered as it dripped out of the latest capsized shells of nearby abandoned buildings like glitter. There was no explanation as to why this tower had stood available to any of the survivors holed up in it.

There were fewer outsiders left to make the trek to the north tower to load up lately anyway. Tenants stopped being allowed outside without guards weeks ago, serviced first by the only rations station still standing within miles in the bottom of the building.

"For your own good," she whispered to herself, wincing at the memory of being blocked from the last walk she'd really needed to take alone to keep herself straight in all of this.

She shook off the reverb and headed towards the kitchen. Out of the corner of her eye she saw three of the balls of paper had been knocked out of the straight line she'd left them in the night before.

Without a word, she went to the kitchen, grabbed a black bag, put the balls still against the mirror in it and took them down to the incinerator.

When she came back the smell of memories of her childhood second cup of coffee triggered a craving for her first of the day.

She grabbed the mug and hunkered down on the floor next to the balls that hadn't been burned.

Taking a sip, she picked up the first ball and uncrumpled it up against the mirror before spreading it out on the floor, pondering what else she was supposed to squeeze from it that she'd missed, ambivalent to the scratches of her handwriting glowing in reverse on the glass.

It hit like lightning.

"GOT it!"she crowed, absently dancing her fingers out against the small, reversed palm print on the mirror in gratitude.

"Thanks-" she whispered.

Giddy laughter erupted on both sides of the looking glass for a few sweet moments before the momentum of yet another nameless day had its way with everything falling apart.

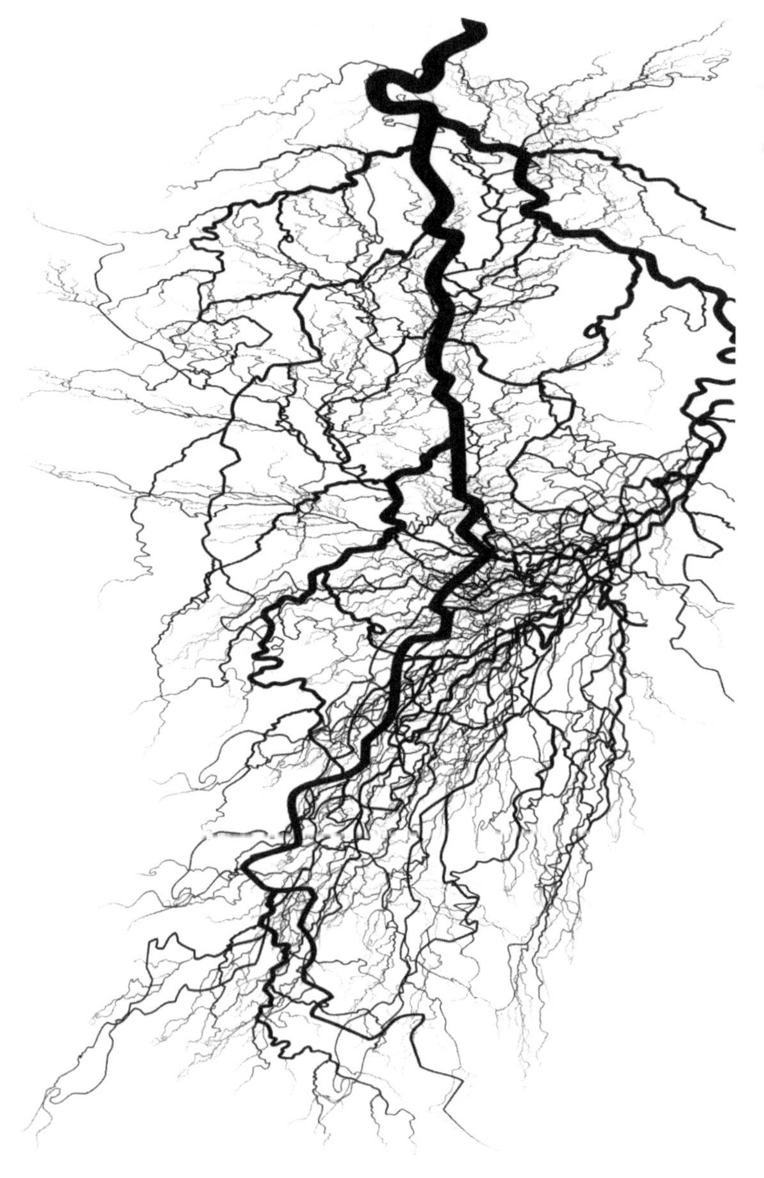

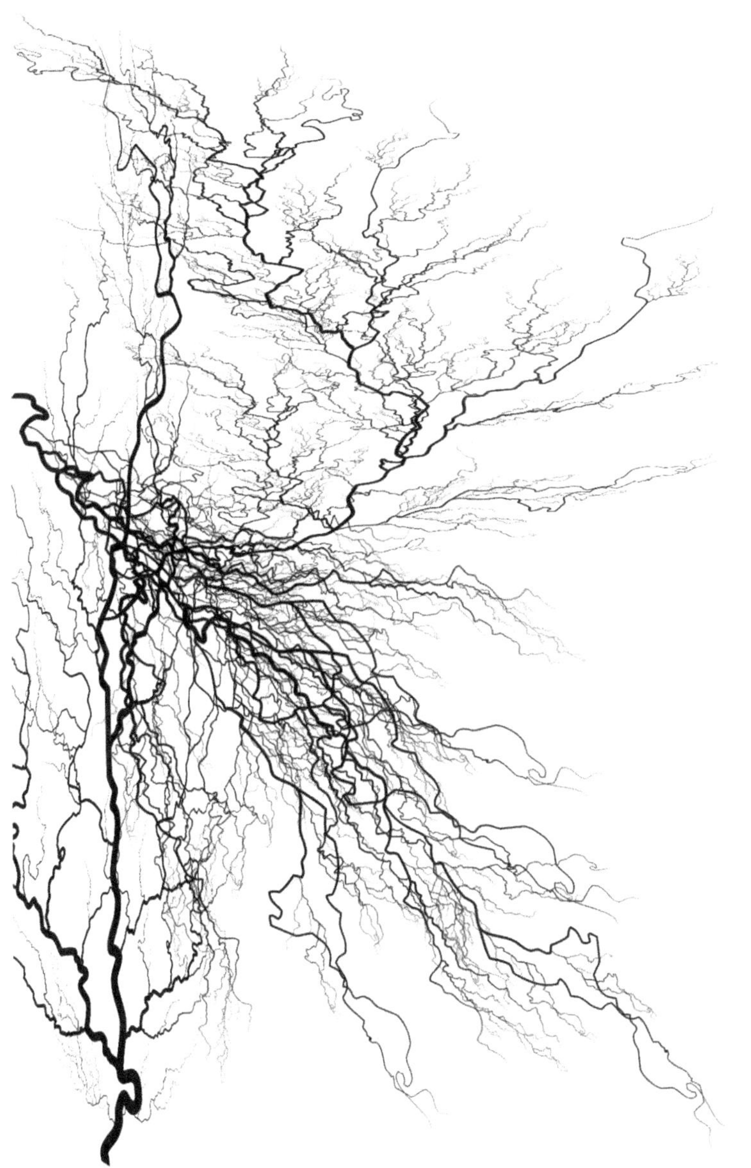

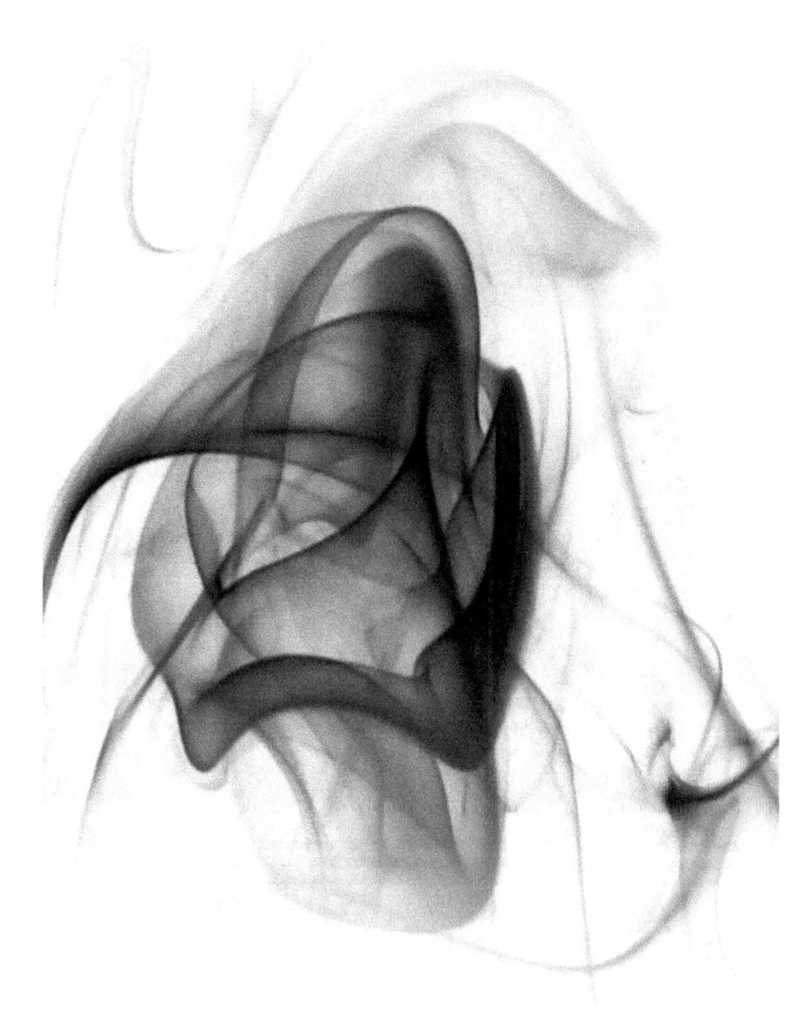

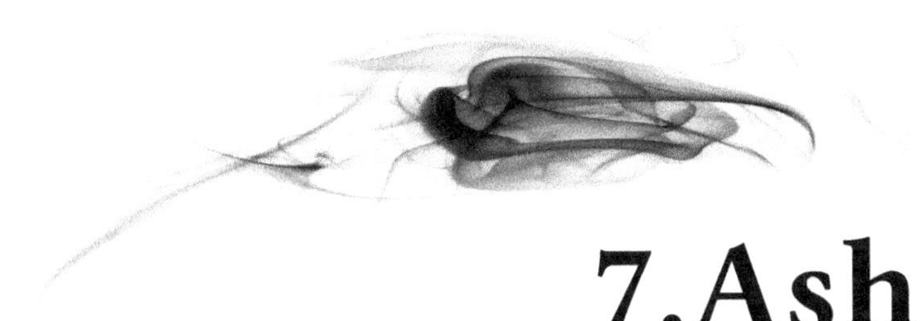

# 7.Ash

"...Eventually, it ends."

She took a sly drag of the first cigarette she'd had in two decades and blew all the smoke out of her mouth like she'd always done.

He looked at her like she was crazy and then grinned.

"You have no idea what you're doing, do you? Give me that-"

He reached for it but she smacked his hand away and half-inhaled again before she pulled the cigarette from between her lips and licked them as the smoke trailed out of the side of her mouth.

"Course I do," she muttered, "I'm not getting addicted to nicotine like you."

She gently placed the last of the cigarette up against his mouth as the pad of her index finger gingerly grazed his lips on purpose.

Momentarily dumbfounded by the lopsided grin beaming out of her eyes and her tongue having wiped away some of the gloss that had hooked him when she'd sat down in the first place, the nicotine brought him back to the issue at hand. He finished what was left of it in one drag, pulled out another and deftly lit it.

She raised a brow as he inhaled damn near all of it, held up his hand as if to say 'one moment,' lit another and wrapped his arm around her shoulders in order to properly position her. "...What are you doing?"she growled.

"Teaching you to inhale, " he whispered into her soft, wild nimbus of hair "and then-"

"AaaGHh-!What the Fuck?!" he screamed and leapt off the lovesest as electricity seemed to snake around the base of his spine and everything broke into pieces.

*

"This is your Pilot speaking, we seem to have made great time and will be arriving at our gate shortly. Please return all seats to their upright position and-"

The curt lilt to the Pilot's polite prattling pulled him the rest of the way out of whatever he'd fallen into due to the subliminals seeping into his system on a loop through the patches behind his ears and synching with what was in the sublinguals he'd dropped under his tongue before take-off. He rammed his thumb up against his brow bone and waited for the vertigo he'd fought for years to return with the pull of gravity on his bones during descent.

Entire body tensed, his armpits were wet by the time they landed. "But no vertigo-" he whispered to himself as the plane emptied, impressed.

He was halfway out of the terminal when he realized he hadn't instinctively patted himself down and slid the cigarette he'd always needed after flights between his lips. He paused. Patted his chest consciously for the first time ever, only to find no pack there. He was walking again before he even noticed.

It was when he hit the unrecycled, humid air outside that he remembered the demented smile shooting out of her eyes, then her outright refusal to stain her pristine lungs with anything but his secondhand smoke mid-act. It was the only time she liked him defiling his lungs. Because it gave her a fighting chance. Everything happily stiffened across the surface of him as he hurried home.

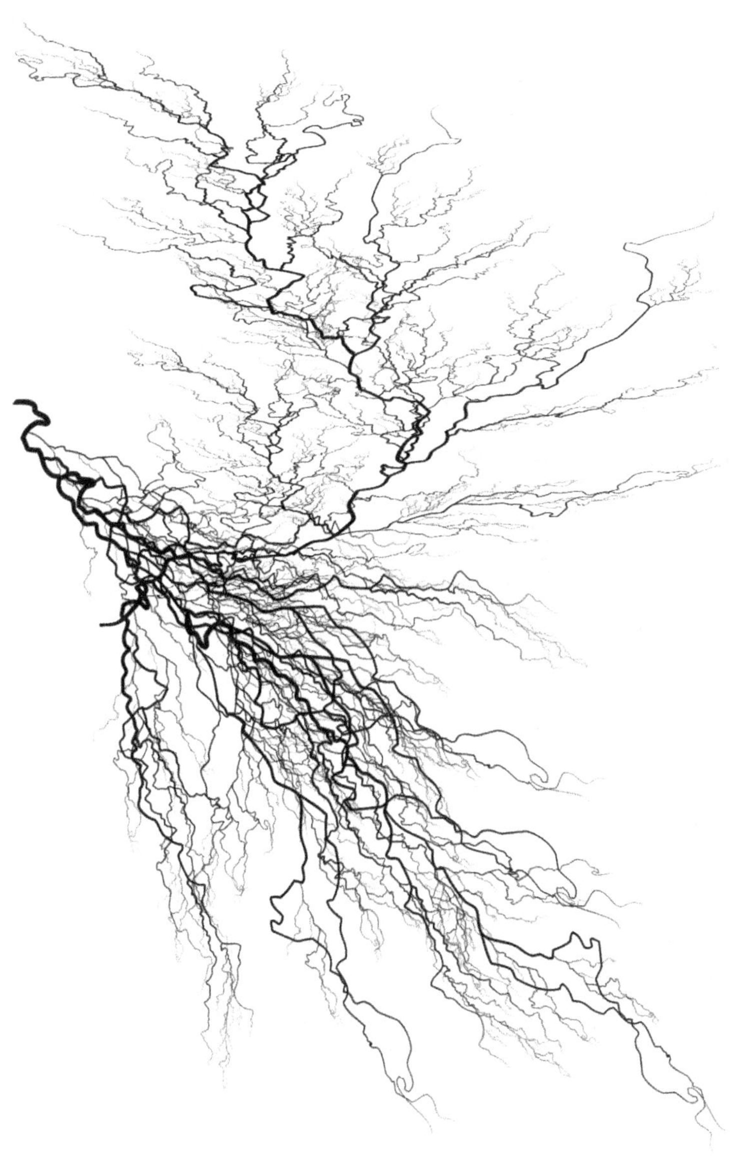

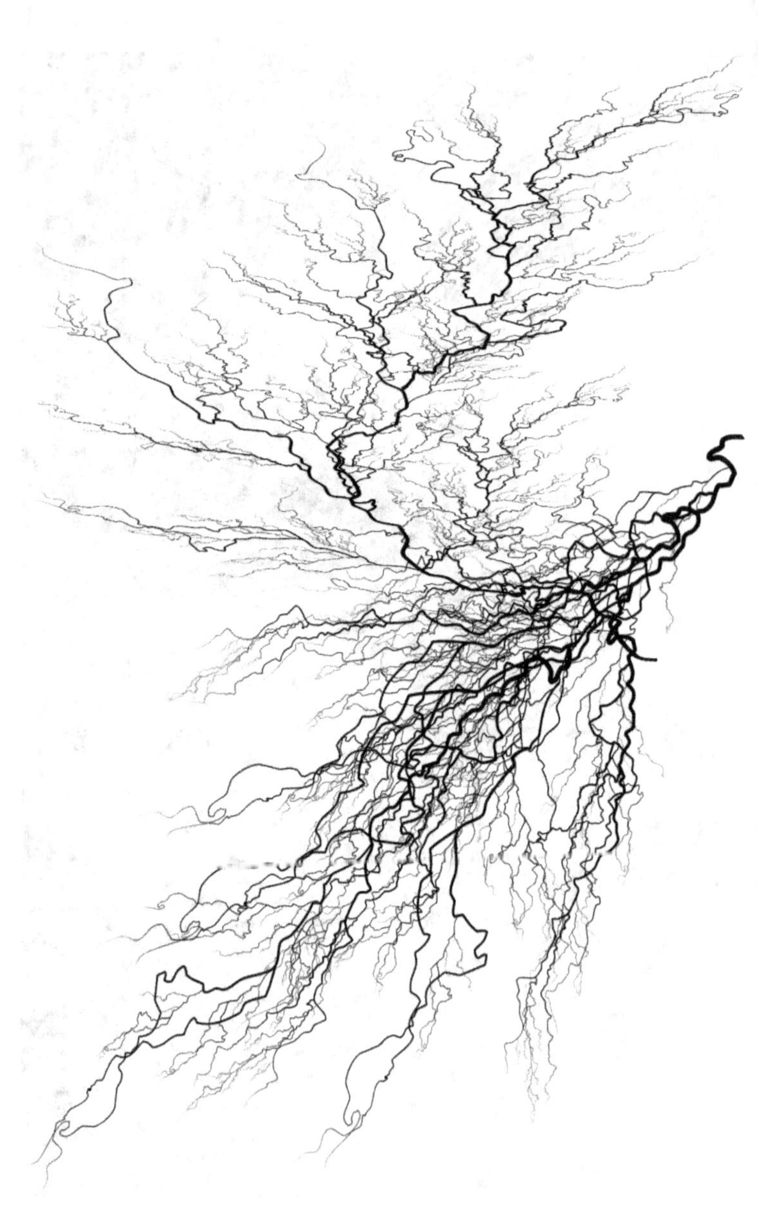

# 8.crave

On instinct she went for her device in the dark but recoiled when her fingers brushed against it.

"Just... to know what time it is, " she muttered.

"Early- the sky is still purple, leave it fucking be-"

She sighed and inched her hand away from it.

His fingers danced along her extended arm affectionately in the dark.

"You told me to do this," he warned.

She winced as he reached past her fingertips, roughly ripped the charging device out the wall and winged it across the room. It landed against the couch with a thud.

His eyes sparkled as she turned to face him." ...Good?" She gently bit him as her reply, eyes tearing up. "GOOood~"he yawned and promptly fell back asleep wrapped around her.

She swiveled around in the dark until she was comfortable in his embrace, staring up at the ceiling. What had shaken her awake from the fucked dream lay pressed to it, waiting for her to close her eyes again.

"I see it-" his soul muttered softly against her cheek, otherwise completely dead to the world. "If it comes for you again, I'll rip everything out of it that it's trying to torture you with. Now go to sleep."

It heard every word he said and glared down on them, alarmed. She blinked slowly and it disappeared.

Face tilted, she tersely kissed him on his nose.

"Yeah, yeah,yeah-" his soul whispered right before the Latent rest of him woke all the way up in the middle of the night.

"You good?" he yawned again as he nuzzled her and protectively twisted her deeper into the freshly laundered sheets as she started to softly protest. Her deeply hued, oiled limbs glistened in the dark to him as much as his glowed to her.

"You took too long to answer! Come here-see, if you wouldn't squirm away we'd both be sleep- "

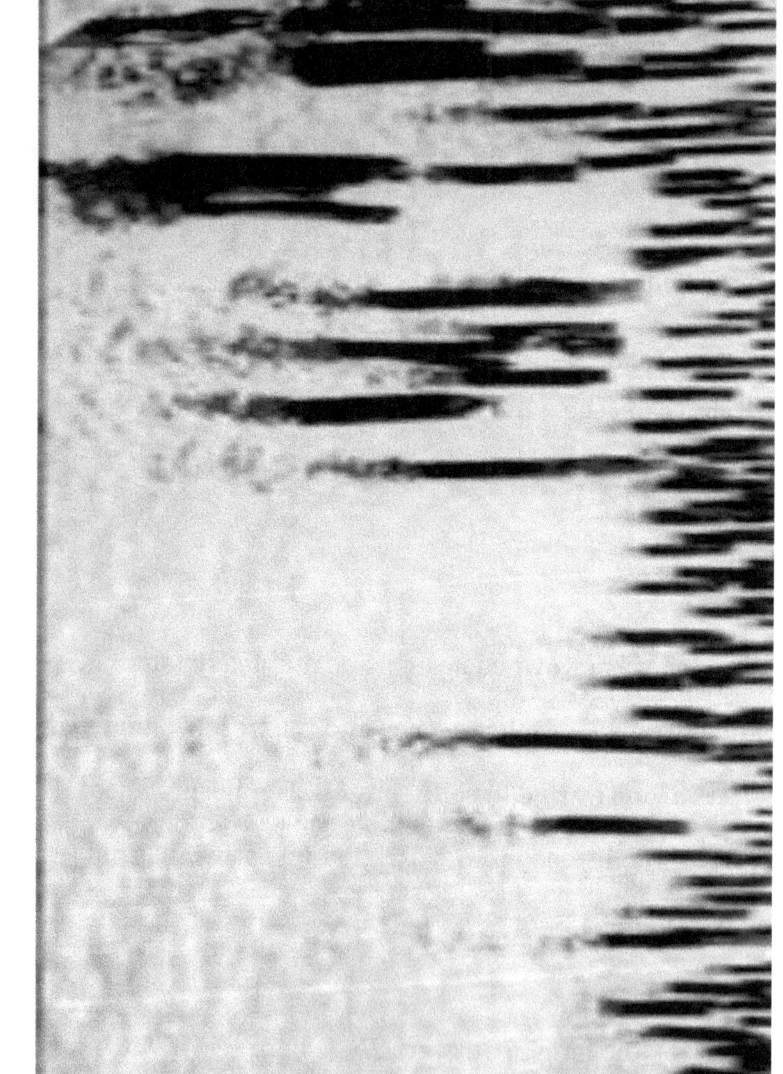

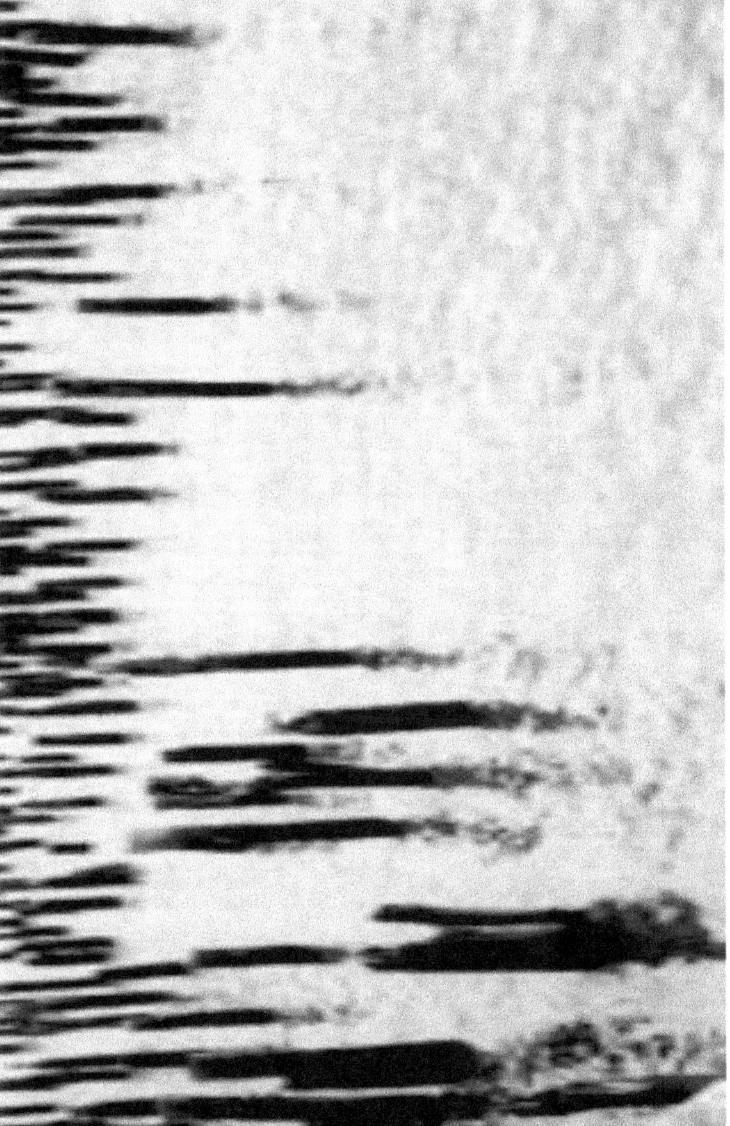

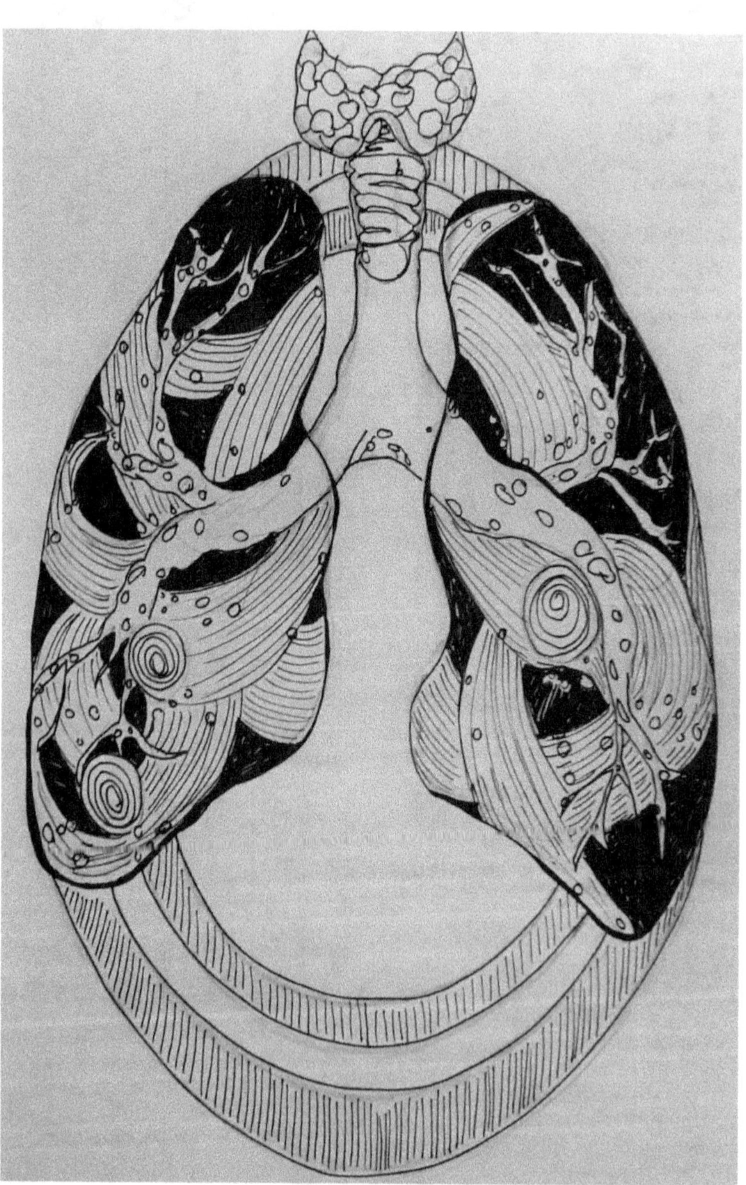

# 9. Sentinels

Everything howled around them.

"I DON'T THINK I can do this for much longer-" she coughed.

"You have to. WE have to. Or all is lost- And it can't be yet... so get it to- " he cocked his head to the side, agitated. "What is up with that wind?" he yelled.

The howling was incessant, metallic almost, and out of key with the rest of nature showing out around them as they kept guard.

"That's not the wind, it's the wind blowing-" she yelled the old axiom back as a joke, trying to not choke on the thick, black smoke churning around where the sentinels were rooted as it lapped at them malevolently.

Lightning exploded silently overhead without the warning of thunder. It made the infernal infrared night gleam with scattershot streaks of blue like an underground, indigo strobelight erupting across a sky stuck on sunset for weeks on end.

They froze.

"Maybe all already is Lost" she said softly, as spooked by the absent thunder as he was.

"I've never seen it this angry," he muttered more to himself than anybody else, in awe as the lightning strikes he counted on autopilot continued to ricochet across the belly of the fog above them, then abruptly stopped.

"Oh my God. It's 440. On the nose-" he barked, horrified.

"Wait- What? 440?! That's impossible- That doesn't make any-" she looked up at the sky, bewildered. Until it started to sink in. "NO! No way-it can't be! It Can't-"

His face darkened as fury rose up from the depths of him. "It's not...IT. It's... THEM!"

"But why would they do That- To-to their own-" she stammered, confused. He raised up to silence her as he instinctively counted off under his breath.

"438,439...and-"

*!wham!*

Another round of an impossible number of lightning strikes slashed out of the overcast underbelly of the sky that both elementals counted, teeth bared.

She pursed her lips. The angry, cracked vertical lines of a woman always surrounded by smoke and snuffing out cigarette stubs cut into her in the shadows as the truth became impossible to ignore.

"It never operates on 440 beats. NEVER. Only the Saturnian sickness in them does when they are lost in their consumptive death march- That's it! They've never appreciated any of this! & we all know it! I'm done. I'm too old for this shit- we all are and we all know it-"

A rustling of outraged agreement danced through the tops of sentinel trees overhead. They looked back towards everything they'd been holding themselves up and away from, trying to protect to the best of their ancient abilities, finally seeing the monsters below for what they truly were.

After millennia of fighting against it, in the quietest moment of the blaze they collectively decided to give the people what every move they made had always shown they really wanted.

The trunks of the trees that housed their spirits entwined branches as another round of programmed electrical mayhem strobed the smoke filled forest they stood rooted in the midst of, leaving behind a dank, dry silence as the remote controlled army of weather machine drones set themselves back to one in the clouds overhead.

The tribe of elementals counted off in the middle of Armageddon together. "435, 436, 437, 38, 39-"

*!wham!*

A whirlwind of electrified strikes slammed into the two lead sentinels and their eucalyptol soaked bodies burst into flames.

A wail of indescribable defiance roared out of their kindred and snaked through their roots and leaves as tree after tree fell, exploding like dominoes rigged with dynamite in the closest to an old growth eucalyptus grove the region had.

Flames shot up into the sky, almost scorching a mechanical wind machine pretending to be divine as the river of fire the elementals had been holding back took the hill through the breach and cascaded down towards the settlement.

*seed.

*time.

...*Harvest.

When the damage was all done there was nothing left for miles but soot, a scattering of scorched yet still standing Eucalyptus on the outskirts of the mostly overturned grove and splinters of charred, barely recognizable human bones.

And seeds.

...Seeds that only opened in instances of hell-like heat prior to pyrophilic pollination.

The shiva-sitting, ash-streaked spirits of the immortals who'd protectively inhabited trunks within that landscape for millennia condensed just enough to be of use on the grounds their eternal hearts gave out on.

They gingerly levitated seeds that had opened like popcorn up off the ground as their divine kamikaze brethren tumbled out of the heavens and caught the seeds up into the sky, taking them where they'd be needed next.

The elementals would find them. Eventually. No matter where the seeds eventually called home. They always did. Across time. Since forever.

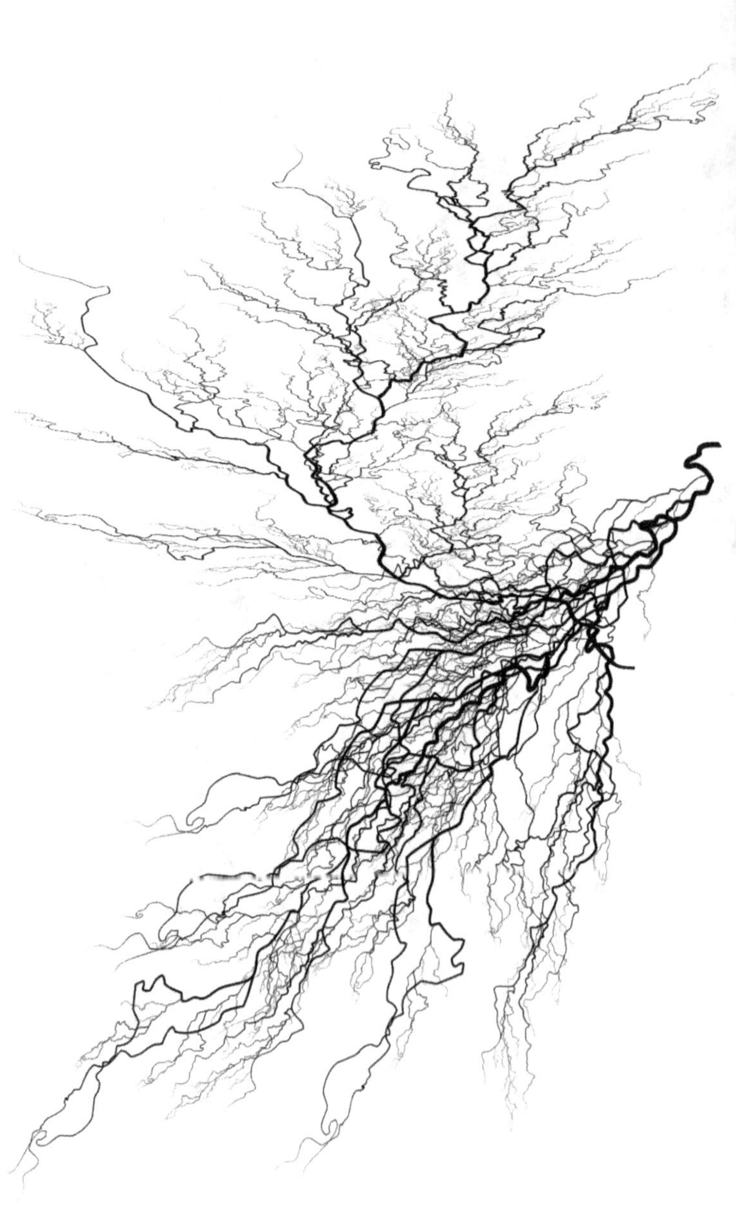

# 10.happiness

He reached for her in the dark.

Nothing but sheets.

Groaning, he opened his eyes.

She was on the ceiling again. Cheek pressed to the carved plaster. Dead to the world.

He stood up sleepily on the bed, wedged his hand between the ceiling and her belly, pulled.

She elbowed him in the face in her sleep.

"SONAFabitch!"he screamed as he crumpled back to the bed and fell hard onto the floor. Cursing under his breath, he lumbered into the bathroom and washed the blood off before he wadded up tissue and angrily rammed it up his right nostril.

Exhausted, he went into the kitchen and grabbed the broom.

When he got back to the threshold his Angel was cascading softly back towards the bed, yawning. Smiling like a little black baby Jesus.

He narrowed his eyes.

In a flash he jumped onto the bed to wake her up, roughly tackling her half-sleep body, pinning her lethal elbows down.

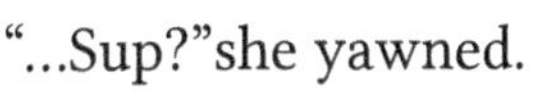

"...Sup?"she yawned.

He yawned back and shifted so all his weight was on her.

She groaned.

"It's for your own good!" he argued, glaring at her.

"Your ears are smoking, Euda" she whispered as she yawned.

"You elbowed me in the nose again, Emonia."

She chuckled darkly. "Maybe if you'd make up with Him so you can come home all the way our magnetic fields wouldn't repel each other soon as we're konked-"

"I'm not mad at- He's doing it on purpose-" he growled.

She kissed him gently on his nose. Everything in him softened. They cuddled wordlessly for a bit.

A nervous thought silently rippled across the surface of him.

"What?"she groaned, knowing what was next.

"I'm not-" he fussed. She groaned again.
"I'm not getting weird, it's just-stop sighing! Look…is he using you as bait to-"

She locked eyes with him. They both turned to water."…bring you back in?"

He nodded nervously.

"You're asking am I BAIT?"

"Yeah."

"This late in the-"she argued.

"I didn't think to ask before! LOOK-nevermind!"he fussed and guiltily shifted so she was not weighed down by him.

The wounded, vulnerable, panicked look in his eyes as he looked away stilled her. She sheepishly let her body levitate gently back up against his instead of floating away. Her lips brushed his temple as her voice echoed in his inner ear.

"I'm not BAIT," she growled, "I'm just... kinda legally AWOL, extended by choice~" she muttered. He craned his head up to look in her eyes.

They gleamed with confusion the same way they had

when she'd saved a prepubescent him from disaster more than half his life ago. Before she'd decided to be born. Again. One last time. For this chance. With him. Again.

She looked away shyly.

Because he freaked out everytime it registered. Whether she was freaking out about it all or not. & it comically got on her nerves. She started to fuss.

" This is just like the song thing! You get so worked up, thinking things mean things bigger than- they do to me because You feel all ephemeral, & kick up all kinds of protective "danger will robinson, girls are sticky!" nonsense to drown out your own tenderness in the first place! & it's just like Ugh! Sometimes a cigar is just a- it's not a big deal~ it's- don't make a big deal outta- stop freaking out... just relax- it's nothing-"

"Said the love who levitates in my arms," he groused, "Sure~everything's fine and normal... none of this lightness of being stuff is out the ordinary at all~"

"At least it isn't Prague, Euda."she muttered, blowing the last of the smoke out of his ears as they pressed into one another.

"Mwahmwahmwah, Emonia."

Happiness entwined, they fell back asleep, weighted blankets twisted around them both.

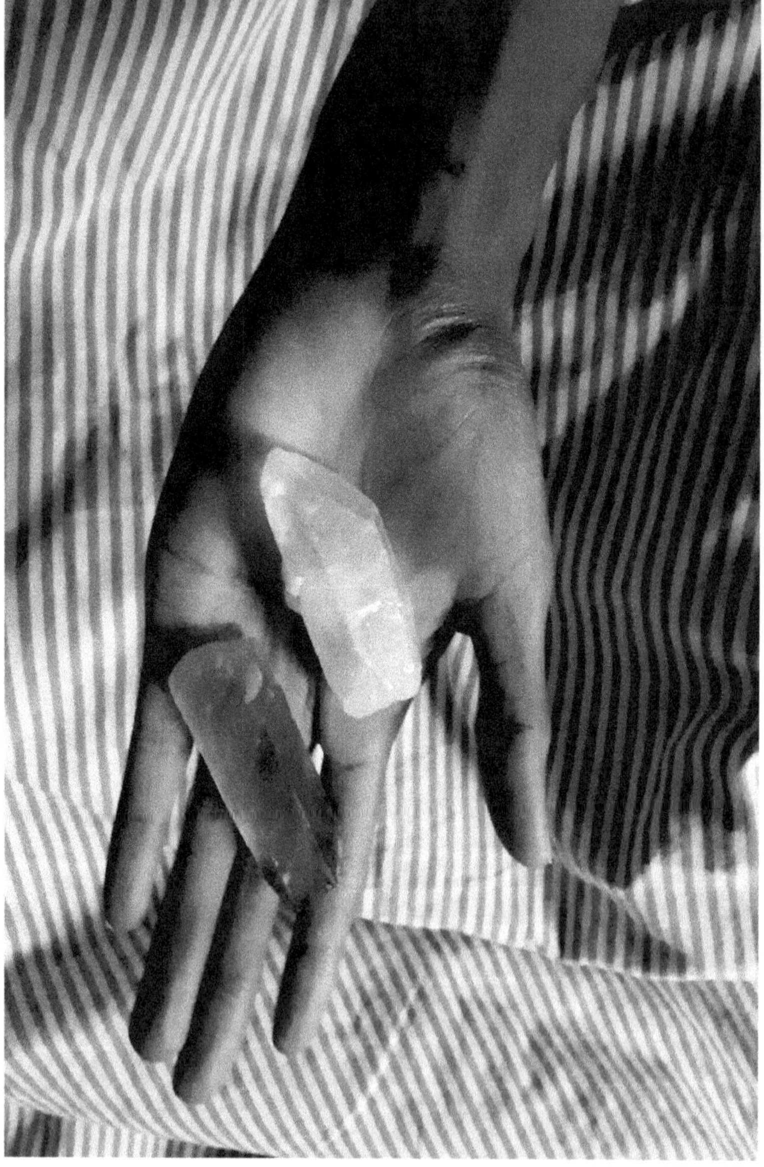

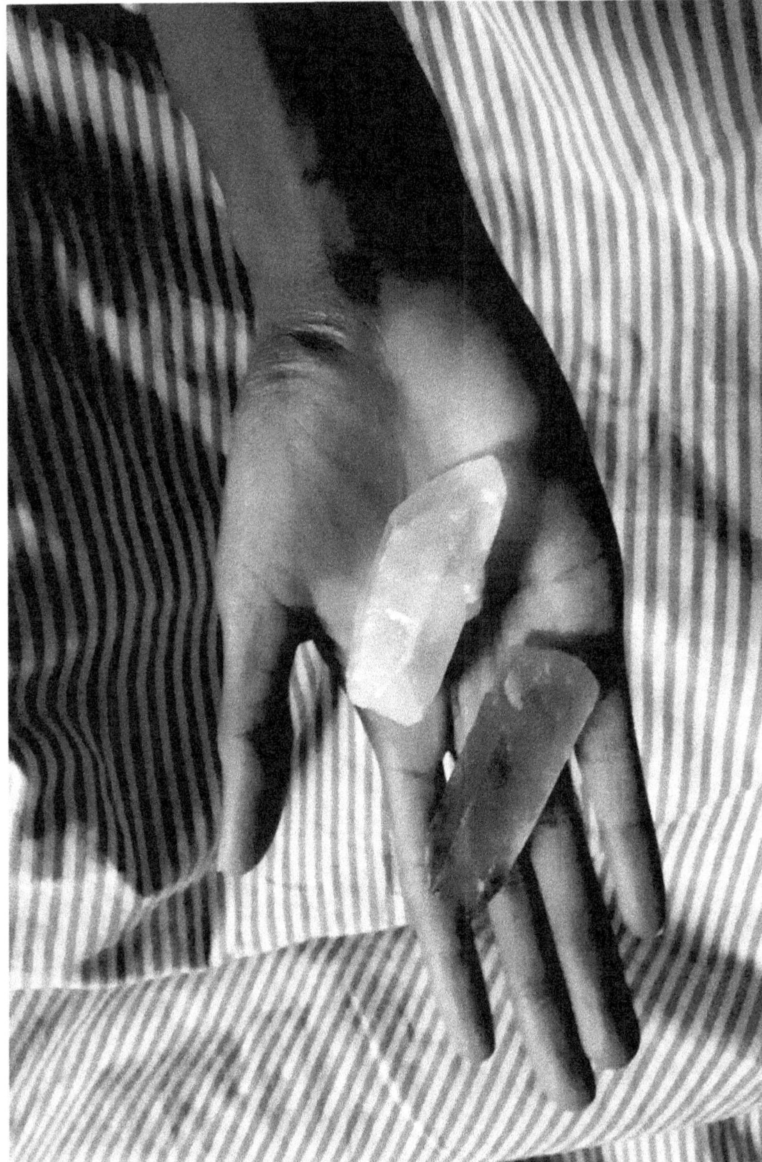

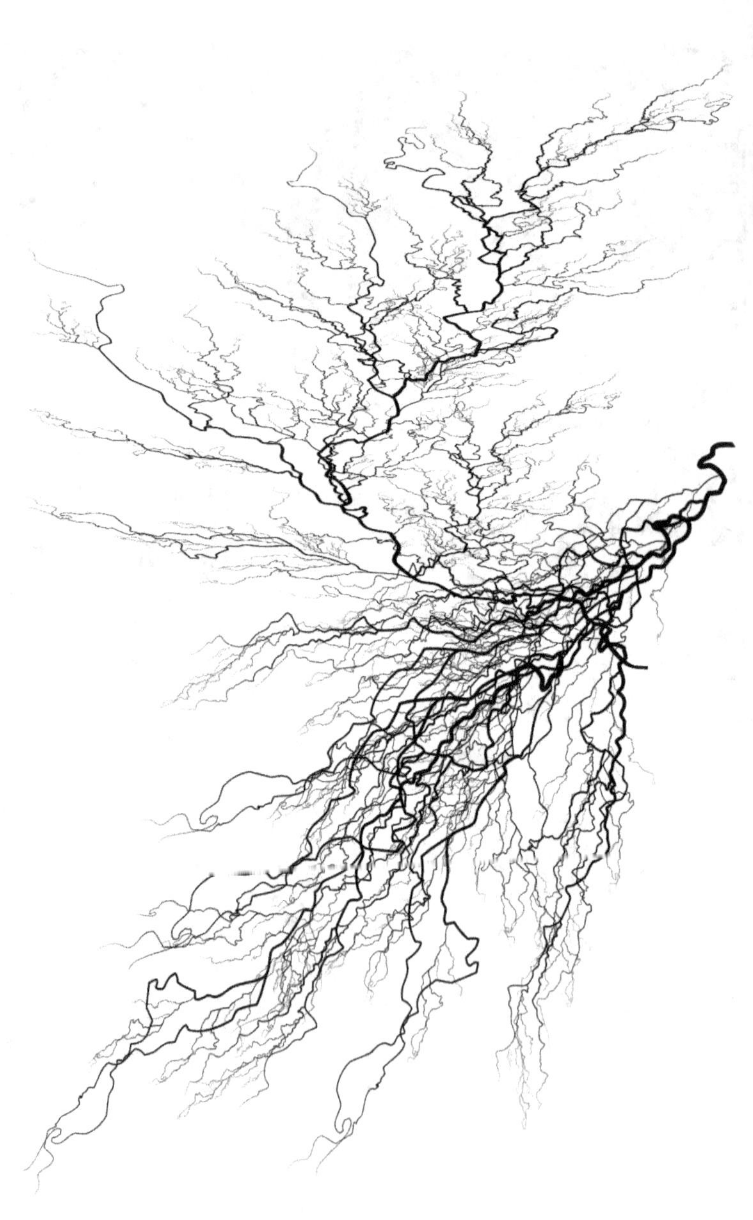

# 11. Lycee

She woke to the sound of glass crunching under his bare feet as he crossed the threshold.

"Fuck!"he screamed. He leaned against the doorjamb and cradled his bleeding foot in his hand.

"What the fuck did you do?! How the fuck didn't I hear any of this? " he muttered, looking around at the destroyed space as he hobbled over to the nearest chair in nothing but his boxers.


She sat up and glared at him from the center of a protective circle made of every glass he'd had systematically crashing to the floor. Her red eyes went as black as the bruise on her arm from last night. She watched him wince as he gingerly picked at the shards in his soles. He yelled as she willed the splinters in deeper in her mind's eye.

"FUCK-Stop it! What are you doing with that fucking gift of yours?!-"he roared and lunged towards her.

She raised her hand.

The ring of broken glass surrounding her levitated and slammed into every square inch of bare skin he had, slicing him like ribbons.

He crumpled to the floor in shock.

She walked over and leered at him as he bled out before moving out of his line of sight. The click of the gas stove coming on was followed by the sound of someone blowing a kiss. He laid there whimpering because he had no illusions. He knew she was going to leave him there to die.

She walked back into the main area, found her things and spat on him.

So there would be DNA evidence.

The smell of gas bloomed around them both. She leaned over his shell shocked frame, sneering.

"I told you I was 15...and you got aroused, you sick fuck. I warned you to let me go-"

He groaned as blood from the lacerations on his eyelids slid down his cheeks like tears.

"Actually," she laughed darkly, "I was 15 when it happened. Your big brother. & it...stunted me. Broke something in me

... that I've decided not to repair. Gave me this...gift... that just keeps on...giving." She looked down at her hands bemusedly as his shit went flying each time her fingers cut through the atmosphere.

The sound of his own blood glugging out of gashes all over him was the only thing he heard beside her monotone voice.

"I'm 24 now. And I'm going to kill every one of you that stood by and watched that night. You're number two. Should've stayed in touch with your high school friends," she whispered.

His outrage at having been lied to about her age stole the pleasure he'd gotten forcing himself on her the night before away from him. It brought him back up to the surface just enough to smell the gas as she slammed the door behind her.

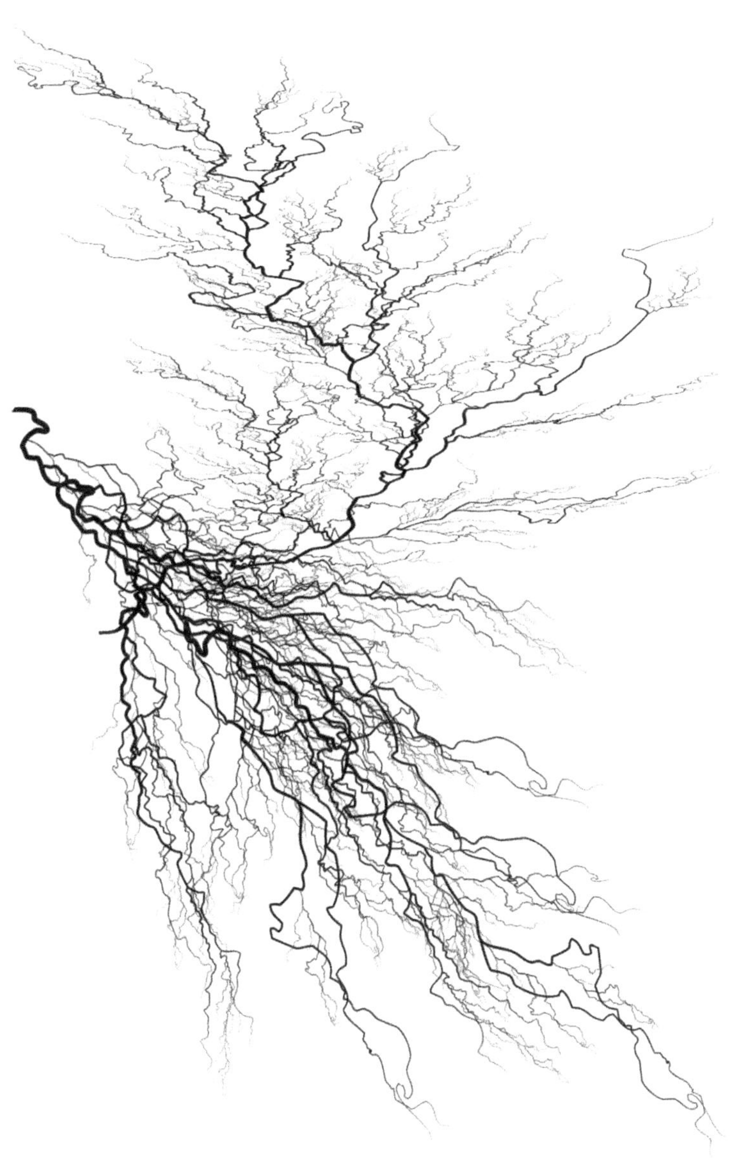

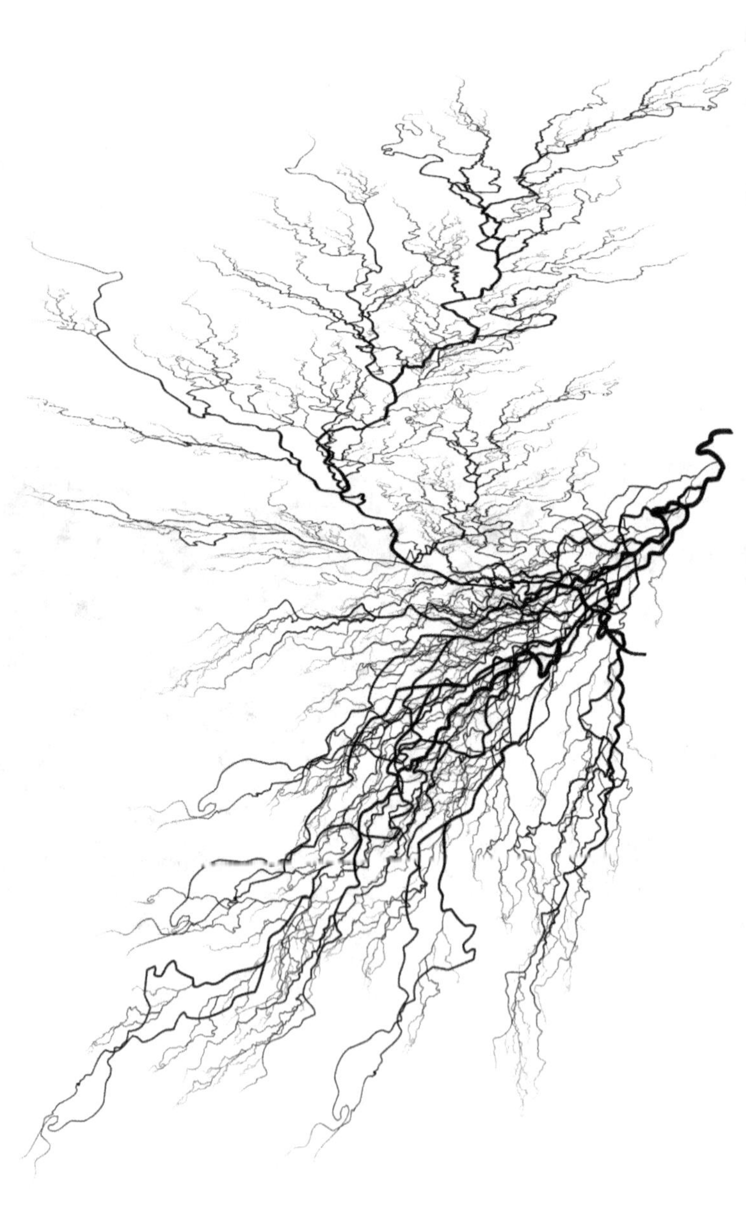

# 12. Pack

The wind howled.

It filled the spaces her screams would have clogged if she didn't have the restraint that she did after he'd done it.

He raised a brow as he paced around her. Like he could tell, like he could hear her responsiveness to him pulsating off of her and was both bewildered and amused by her fighting off being in the throes of it whether she'd ever act on it or not, no matter if anything else around them was cognizant of it or not. The spectacle of it all had damn near thrown her into heat.

He growled, which was bad enough.

The worst thing he could do.


But when the first syllable to escape a mouth he hadn't

even realized was dry cracked, she laughed and stepped

away a bit, the spell broken. Watching her work had made

him parched. Inadvertently showing that freed them both.


They looked away, shook it off and spoke over each other,

trying to gain control of the situation.

"Now what?" they brusquely snapped,

inadvertently in unison. He sized it up.


"Well... since you shot through him and then incorrectly

pistol-whipped him, we could technically leave him here.

He'll come back to in a few as he's bleeding out."

A groan wheezed up from below.

"...Will mountain lions get him?" she asked expectantly, weighing the pros of the path.

The winds kicked up.

"They'd definitely smell him soon enough on a night like tonight." he said. "Or you could aim higher next one and just put him out of his misery-"

She dipped down & rifled through her now wounded old harasser's pockets, grabbed his car keys , split them and threw them in opposite directions.

"Okay, I guess you've made your-" he began but stopped when she shot him in the thigh of the other leg and chuckled darkly.

The harasser called on God then whimpered her name as she stared blankly down at him.

"This is why yer God didn't let you play with guns before, isn't it?" he snarked as he flicked some of the wounded, crying dude's blood off his cheek in disgust.

"Yeah. No mountain lions," she grunted and crouched down over the one who'd totally read her speaking on shit wrong and stupidly kicked shit up again when she'd been Trying to absolve them both.
The bullets had gone clean through.
She scooped up both.

"I said I was sorry, I was coming to say I- I thought you forgave me!" he whispered.

"I know," she whispered back, "but I remembered what you did with my agents to make them not send me out, trying make me starve and...pop-pop~" she shrugged.

"Why didn't you do this shit before?Fuck!! " he angrily cried out.

"So you could raise your son," she said simply," That lil dude's grown now...and I wanted to see if you'd be dumb enough to try it sober, knowing God forgave me 2000+ years before you fucking made these two fucking bullets become necessary...or the mountain lions. But...I forgive you again?"she said sweetly.

He rolled his eyes at her sudden softness. "Scuse me," he interrupted as he reached down, slipped the gun from her hand and knocked her old harasser back out with it.

"See that? The correct way to pistol-whip is to wing it down like so~" he demonstrated. "Try it," he ordered.

"He's already out."she grunted.

He took a swig from his bottle of water and then dashed the rest of the contents into the asshole's face. He came to with a start. She whacked him roughly and smiled up at her mentor like little baby jesus.

"Good!" he barked as the wind kicked up again alongside the faint baying of wolves. She jumped, surprised.

"Oh yeah, forgot they're making a comeback. Just taken off the protected list-They sound nearby, too," he mused "Wanna stick around & watch what gets him first from the truck?"

She nodded happily, skipped over to the steel grey behemoth and scampered in, grabbing a bottle of st. Germaine from the back as he climbed in on the other side and turned on music. Her eyes glistened with joy.

"You know, " he started after a few beats,"maaaybeee you should've just told me that in everything else you fucking decided to cover in your -"

"Where? The cover letter? " she sniffed.
"Yeah, by the way the real reason my resume is sooo erratic is~ like you'd have called, " she muttered.

"Touchè...Point taken," he muttered back.
"But you're blunt as fuck, I figged you'd say what the fuck is up with that? In the in-person one...and I'd have awkwardly explained it." she mumbled.

"Besides, he wasn't the reason why I came to you. He was the reason I didn't chart a course that would've made me a no-brainer to you to take on."she clarified. "He stole...a lot," she said softly then guzzled half the ornate bottle.

"I can't believe he started up again," he muttered, motioned for the bottle, took a swig and made a face ."Ugh-how are you drinking this straight?"

The baying got closer.

"Medicinally," she grinned lopsidedly in the dark cab, "it's made by monks and tonight? This was holy-" she got quiet.

"Thanks," she whispered.

He waved it off gruffly. "I don't have sisters, but if I did... and cops told her she'd go to jail for protecting herself from a dude sending her pics of burn victims modeling bikinis when he'd tracked her across state lines after he'd paid her home agent to block her going for-" he stopped, hearing him shuffle awake on the ground outside.

He turned off the high beams that flooded the place and they sat in the dark and waited in silence. Eight pairs of eyes popped open in the bushes nearby.

"My pleasure," he grunted as the wolves circled the panic stricken guy.

The first wolf lunged and he blew the horn, scattering them a bit, almost giving the guy a heart attack.

He laughed darkly. "Ready?"


She blush-grinned and nodded yes.

"Tell anybody I helped you-" he started.

"I know, I know- the swords" she grumbled.


They drove off in silence as tv on the radio's wolf like me

blared out into the night sky.

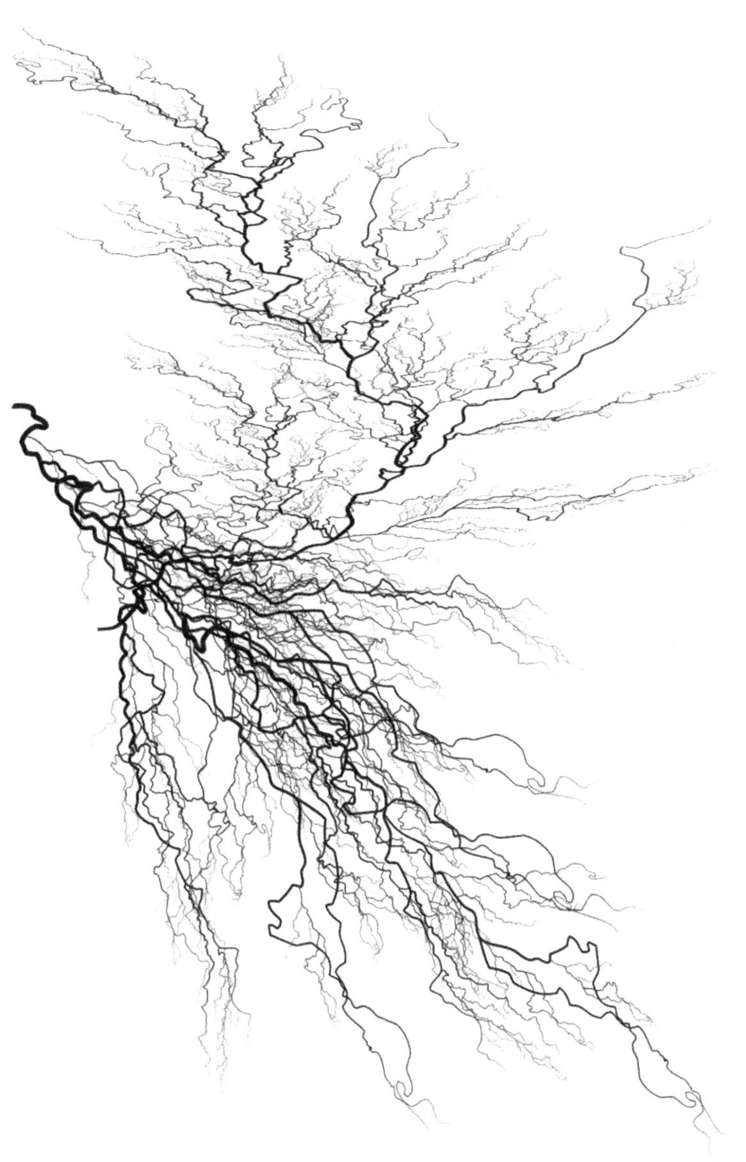

PHOTO
HAIR
PEACE
BED
PEACE

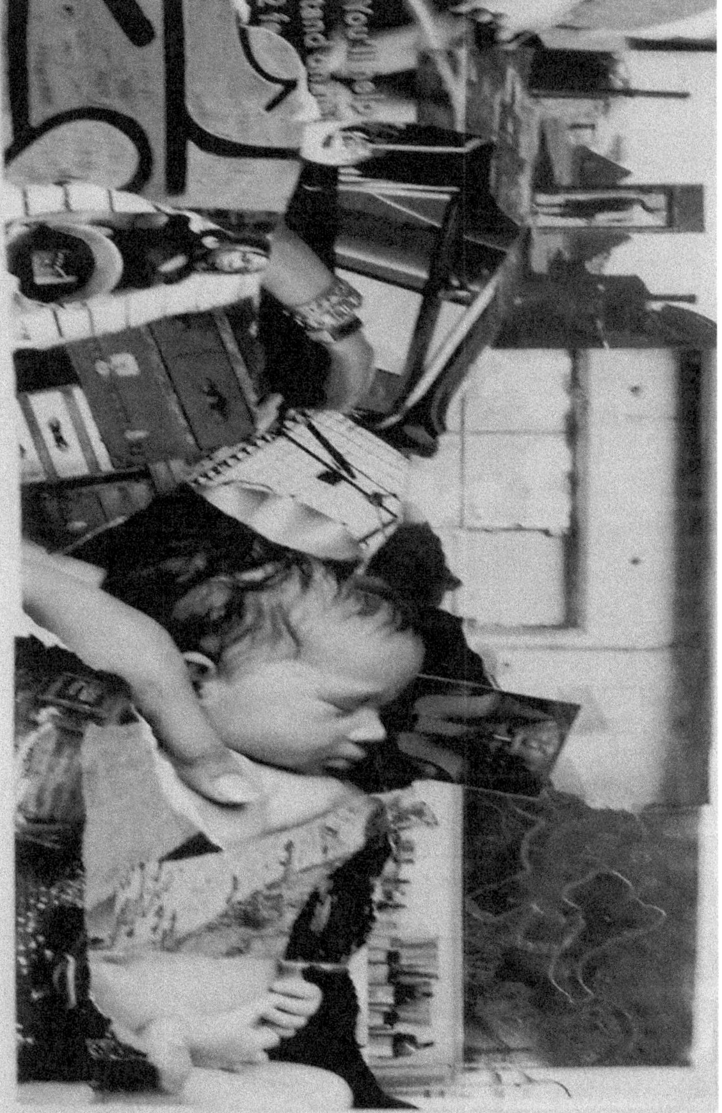

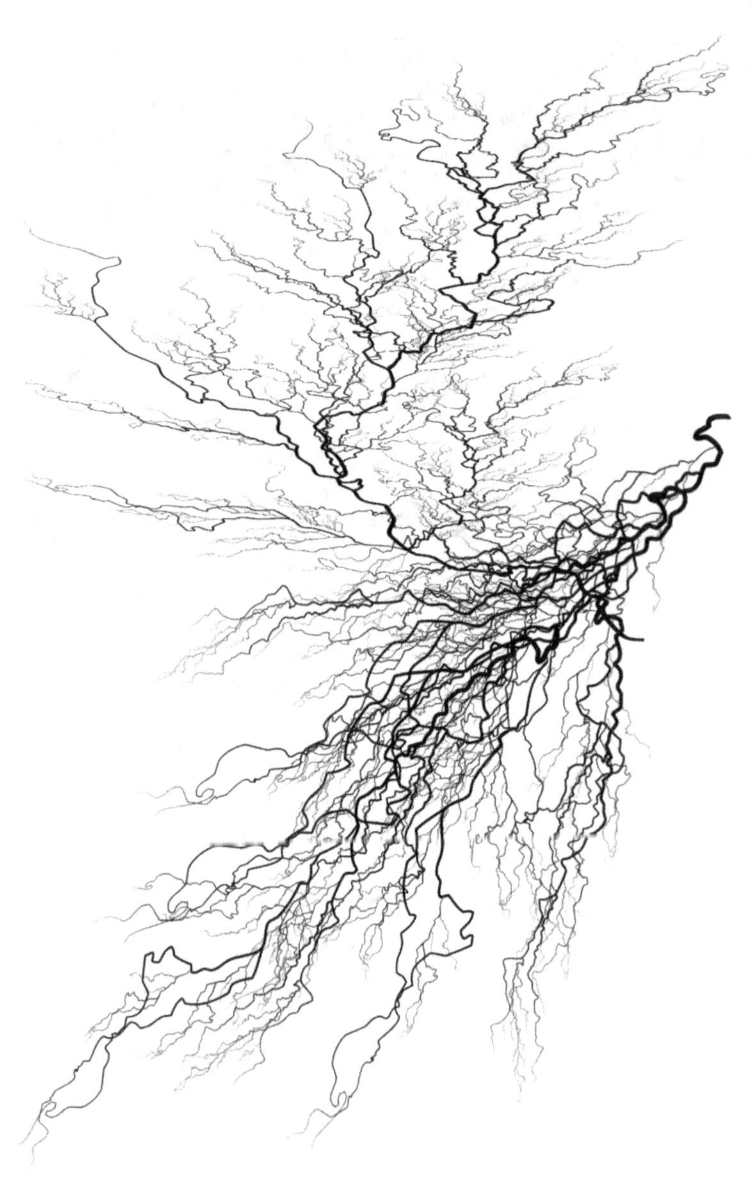

# 13.KIN

She'd paused.

Even though she couldn't shake that this was the place,
that there was something that had to be done from there
that would remain unintelligible until she hit that corner,
something about the profile pic was off in a way she'd not
been able to put words to.

On the cusp of making the 2week reservation she'd
shaved it to five days.

...To move in openness but play it by ear.

*


She arrived after dark due to daylight savings time, a thing
that couldn't have been farther from her mind when she'd

booked. In all her years on the road that had never mattered. This night it did.

After falling asleep in her shades on the way in something about the acrid smell of those casing interlopers unloading made her keep them on as she scoped the place.
At the foot of an outcropping that loomed like a lifeguard hut above a sea of spelled beings she clocked him.

A Guard, guarding.
She walked directly towards him. The intensity of her press in the shell-shocked throngs made her catch his attention instantly.

He gruffly tossed his chin up to kick on his tonebox in case her lilt matched her strangely sharp gait.
"Li-ti- Is where I'm headed safe? Never been in this chunk before," she muttered and held up her hand.

He sighed and winked to click off the box in relief. He never trusted the box's translations. He casually whipped out his black light and scanned her palm so he could see the destination.  She looked sideways at drained bodies shuffling listlessly about that shifted slightly toward her upon seeing her naked wrist.

"Oh…There?" he smiled broadly.
She felt the forms around them flinch back into the shadows due to the force of the UV light that erupted out of his mouth due to his grill. "Yeah!-that's my block! But I wouldn't press through to it in the dark without scoping it in the light, if you know what I mean…"

"Yeah, I do," she chuckled abrasively, raised the index finger of her still outstretched hand to the rim of her shades and slowly pulled them down her nose.

A slash of UV harsher than what his teeth had been set to slid across his face and everything beyond him. The Threadbares that had flinched outright fled from the concourse.

"Ooh~Where did you get those?! Military grade?"
"Nah...originals, Amplifieds. Early ones, before they started designing them to die out on Dtants at the most inopportune moments," she growled.

"Ah yeah, the capitalism of the continually re-up or be killed clause," he chuckled and pointed to his teeth. "These mothafuckers are military. Luckily moms inhaled loads of it carrying me so there's enough residuals in my bones to amplify the... experience-"
"Thought you were an Amph, too" she grinned. "Even though you are youngish in the-"

"Yeah, it's in the sling of my smile they say. Where you're headed? You can walk it… but even I ride it on nights like this," he muttered.

"What's so special about tonight? "
"New shipments due. They keep the peace 'round here by rationing out the feed."

"They…Frenzy? here?"
"Full on. Chosens. Sacrifices, too. Less adrenal ish. Changes the taste. And it's two days late."

He looked around, the light from his soft smile sweeping the concourse behind her with searing light as she stared at his face, trying to guesstimate how young his mother would've had to have been for him to be a latter day original.

"I …feel bad for them, " he muttered. "Not due to choices or faults or blame and shit… the beast do what it do, but…" he paused.

"They are trying so hard… to hold it together. To… not …you know…outside of frenzies. Because they remember. Before, you know? They weren't always Inflicteds." he grunted, "and they get no respect around these parts for the love in… that display of-"

"Restraint?" she offered.
He nodded, knowing she got it."You know… I get off in about an hour. I'm sure word's spread about you through the belly of this place…if you're up for some shellscanning for a bit… there's a promised land cafe over there called Sweetbreads… I'll fly you to where you need to be when I head…home-"

His voice trailed off, almost shyly. It was what made her change her mind.

"They UV up the whathaveyous?"she asked gruffly. His smile broke out of his face like the moon reflecting the light of the sun.

"Course- place is totally veiled. Tell'em I sent you, they'll hook you up even more than they will just for surviving the cross-" he blushgrinned.

"Who are you to them?"she asked.

"Well…Rå, of course," he blushgrinned, beaming. "And who are you … to me?"

She smirked. "NUůt, ironically enough."

She gamely pulled down her cowl. Shards of UV light were scattered like constellations across her glistening coppery flesh.

Rå chuckled. "Knew from how you walked up on me you were kin. Sweetbreads is up the ramp…. I'll yell for you when it's~"

"Yeah, yeah, yeah…and thanks. Ahead of time."she laughed and headed up to the promised land.

"Li-wey," he said more to himself than anyone else as she ambled away.

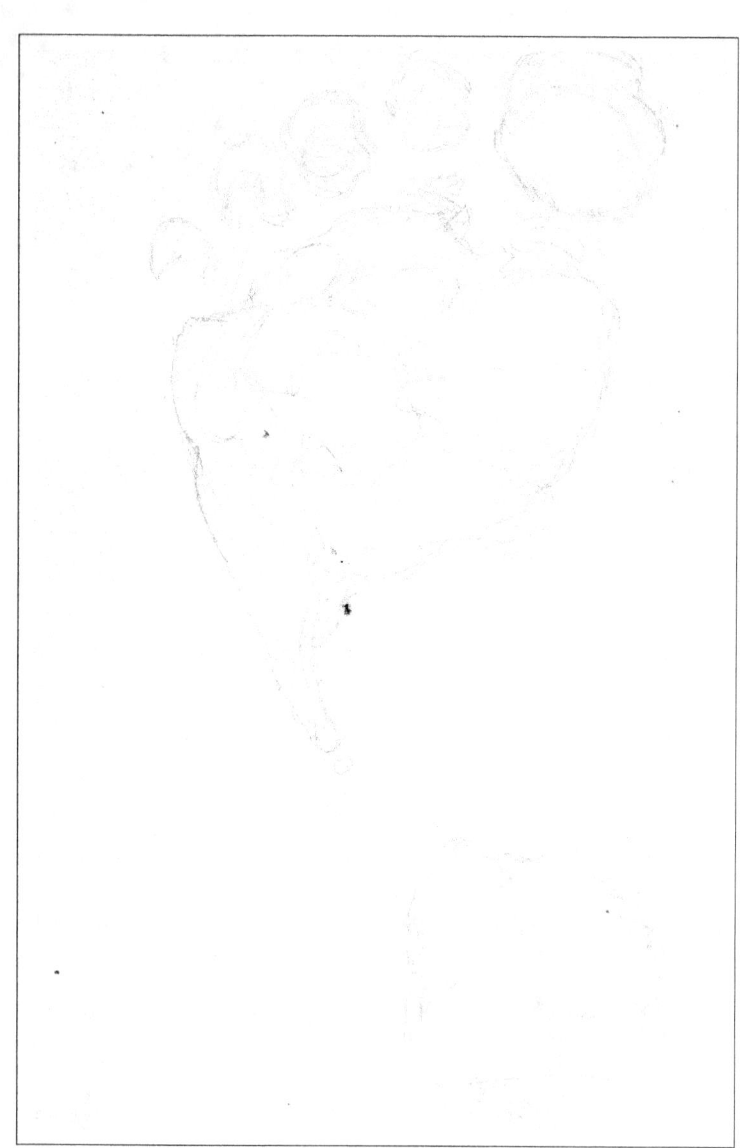

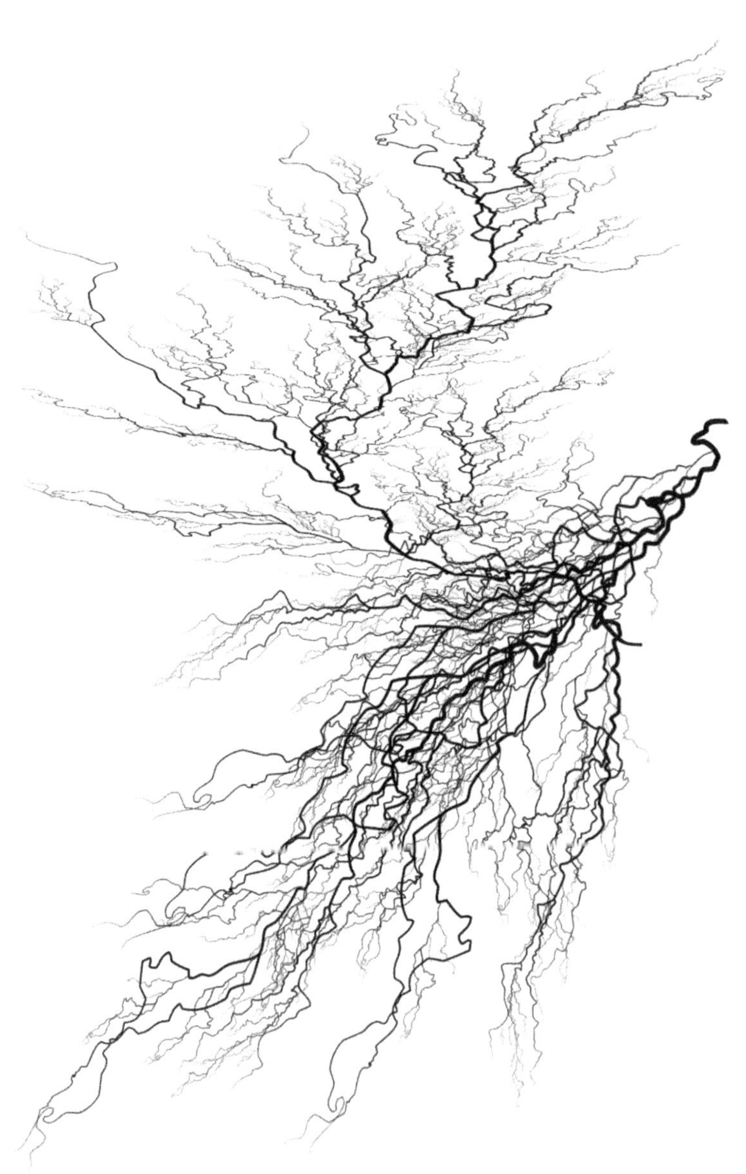

# 14. Ephesus

She didn't hide her bristling against it

under the surface but she stayed

silent. "Wanna talk about it? " he

whispered against the side of her head.

She said nothing. Just stared at the screen balefully.


"They got it wrong, didn't they? " he asked, gauging

her. She didn't seem like she was breathing even

though her flesh felt warm against his bare skin.

"You're...insulted." he concluded.


The rains kicked up outside. The pellets slashed across the

landscape like they were looking for blood, or light, or a power grid to angrily attack in outrage. To end the blasphemy with a show of unmitigated violence against the godless communities that seeped through the hills like an infection.

The blackout hit the area without warning. Weary people hunkered down even deeper in palaces that the plague they'd all gone through feel like hovels and tried to sleep through the storm.

It was only after the thin streak of light cut across the scrim before it and everything else around them went black that he heard her carefully measured breath echo around him again. He exhaled to breathe her in and held on tighter. She stiffened under the weight of his heavy arms and then gave up the ghost, melting into him.

Eons passing were embedded in each syllable that fell

from her lips moments later.

"They always do." she growled. "Get it wrong. But this? This is why we walk away again and again. This? This is spite. They know the truth. They're trying to hide it from those who'll come after them, trying to poison the well of the world against the truth to ensure their own pitiable survival. They have no respect. They don't deserve us. Didn't then. Don't now."

"Which is why things always burn," he murmured against the spirit of her inside his own mainframe.

She pressed her tongue against the sheath that housed his pineal gland and it fully opened. He stammered in his mother tongue as he came all the way online, incoherent to all but her.

"Come up here ~" she growled affectionately and watched with baited breath as he rose into himself alongside her.

He looked sideways at her in her true form and then out over the sea of pizeoelectricity that he'd first found her inexplicably floating in.

"...Feels like forever ago." he muttered.

"Know why you sensed my stance ... to all that?" she asked.

He shook his head no.

"...Because she's you too. Only way you were able to find me."

The lightning storm over his inner sea subsided, calming her down in front of his eyes.

He woke with a start.

He kissed her on the only temple she seemed to bother with this run. She burrowed deeper into his arms, dead to the world as the insipid movie they fallen asleep on blathered on.


...But not to him.

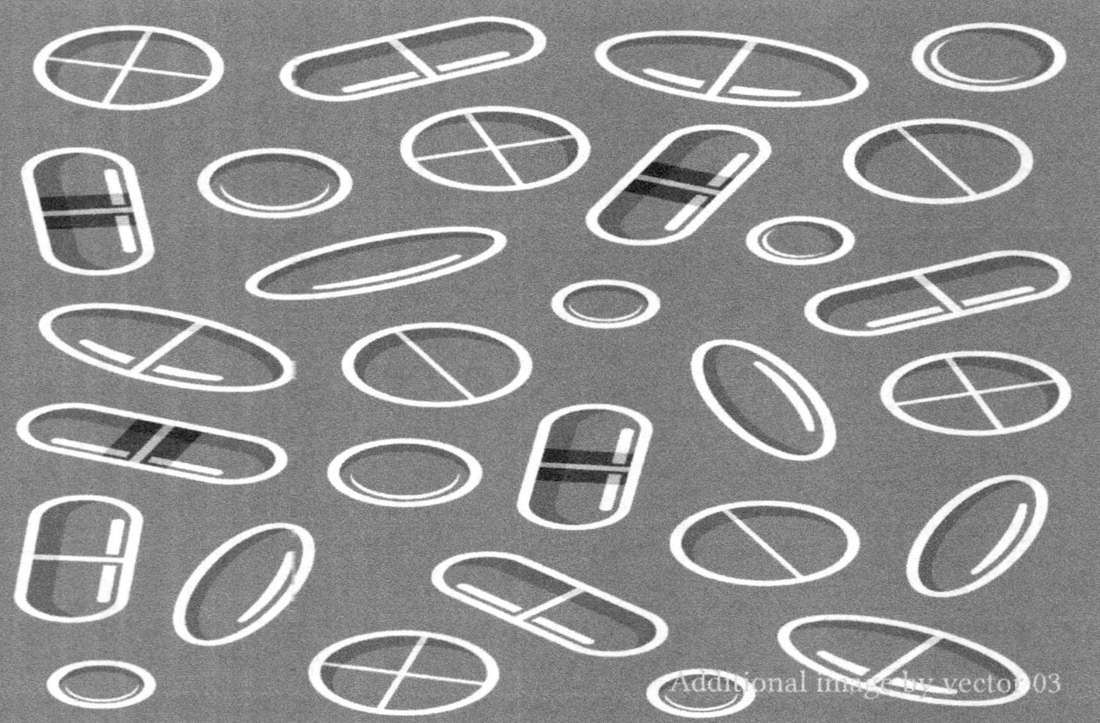

Additional image for vector 03

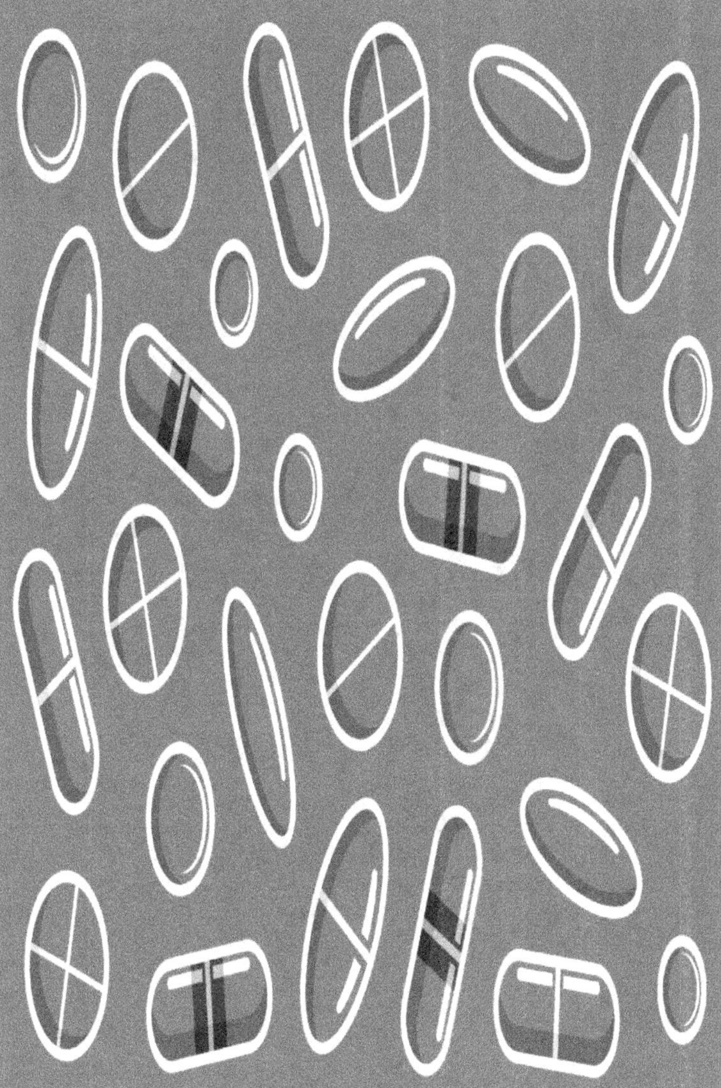

# 15.New World, Braved

With each wheezed inhale between words he leaned more towards the screen, rapt as she wedged herself deeper into the farthest corner of the couch.

Out the corner of her eye she solemnly watched him where he'd always been, even before this began. Her heavily fringed lashes threw shadows across a perfectly made up face right where the bruises from his last post-rally exultation/celebration were hidden.

It was better this way. When she helped him forget.

He was more violent when something about her existence made him remember.

"Fucking commies! Faggots! All of 'em! Fuck them! This land is ours, yeah!" His hand slammed down on the coffee table with such ferocity that the entire room shook.

She ran off to the bathroom and then quietly made her way towards the back door, dropping her keys.  All the color drained from her face as the noise drew the smog in him directly to the scent of fear coating her. He was leaning casually against the doorjamb before her fingers had lifted back off the floor.

"Going somewhere? " he asked, inebriated by the toxic power-trip he'd inhaled digitally alongside his brothers."Stay down there, "he growled authoritatively. She froze. "Answer me! Where the fuck do you think you're-"

"Groceries! Grocery-sh-shopping- it's Tuesday and... you picked Tuesday nights to-" she stammered. "You're almost out of beer, the new shipment arrives on Tuesdays, remember-"

He grunted, rolled his eyes and made his way to the fridge. "Don't you fucking move!"he snarled. "Just my luck! We finally get all the niggers, chunks, faggots, fucking libtards and Mexicans out of our land... and it seems like me and all my boys are still having to deal with the same ignorant bullshit now seeping out of our dumb blond bitches too! You worked alongside those motherfuckers too damn long! You just soaked their stupidity up, didn't you?! It's gonna take God knows how long to beat that outta-"

He finally opened the fridge and saw two lonely golden tower beer cans with the etched relief of a solid gold crapper stamped on them. His mouth went momentarily numb and his thoughts turned to mush.

She knew the pause and took her chance, slipping out the back door, diving into her gun-racked SUV and plowed down the drive.

He came out of his stupor to the sound of cheers over the greatest display of manhood he'd ever seen in his life coming back for part two of his state of the union address, grabbed the last two cans and plopped back down in his favorite chair, the one that made him feel like he was right there.

He cracked open the laces can, gulped half of it down. The little blue bruise on his wrist where his recently recalled brethren fitbit had been blinked and the world around him dissolved.

*

She'd watched the private nightmare she'd lived in, had even gotten to the precipice of escaping, turn into nationalistic new normal where they were. Days that had turned to weeks and months due to the plague their bubble ignored bent back and strangled any peace she found in moments like these away from him.

After steadying herself behind the wheel she made her way into the store.

Coughing cashiers counted out change in a line behind her as she pushed into the harried crush of made up wives and girlfriends who'd also figured out when the trucks came in and had slipped the Intel into their men so they could take credit for outmaneuvering their brothers and keep the peace.

She was unable to ignore the broken looks in the eyes of women just like her alongside the despotic men they had cheered onto finally having their way at the cost of everyone else, only to become the targets of the snakes they'd fed with no minorities left in range.

She loaded up on overpriced, subpar products stamped with the golden tower logo, teetering as she wedged case after case of ironically shitty beer on the bottom shelf of her cart next to the gold flecked toilet paper the followers had demanded as proof of life that they too were part of the family.  She wracked her brain trying to recall how long ago it'd been since a brand other than the golden tower umbrella had been available at any of their outlets. The time he broke her acrylic nail off for trying to protect their daughter from his attacks before the girl ran away flashed before her eyes.

That had been expected, with all the brethren rechristening their daughters with the same name as his daughter as a show of respect.

But not the shortages.

Supposedly triggered by private companies exercising their right to choose to not service hotbeds of domestic terrorism in areas the bubble's now cleansed news continually reported as Paradises onto their heads, the same intel that proved to be true regarding the shipment days claimed the shortages were designed to be implemented from the top to take care of pesky surpluses of dead stock within the tower's vastly shrunken distribution channels.

She stood there mystified at how time had seemed to stop and had fled at the same time. Just like the gardeners, the clerks, much of the working class in general across the color lines.

Of course, new people were always coming into the bubble. The Rv checkpoints were so backed up in the three directions that raucous, mask-free border towns had sprung up that were policed by spraying hazmat-suited agents atop the outer walls they'd already been let past.  And since their was such a spirit of camaraderie they flowed right into those promised vacant jobs they'd made the treks for, if little more.

They'd decried the socialist turns of society in the past for lumping them in with undesirables but here, in paradise, they were all in this together. Like an aryan family.

The noise behind her pulled her out of her thoughts. She looked up as men in hazmat gear sprinted by to cordon off where the latest who'd simply not make it back home had fallen as a biohazard formality, shrugged it off and made it to an open cashier.

"What happened back there? " the cashier whispered.

"I don't really care, do you?" she asked flippantly as she lifted her hand and fluffed her bangs.

"Yeah, I do, actually," the cashier replied.
The woman chuckled"... then you're in the wrong place-"

The cashier coldly looked her Sister in arms in the eyes as the woman laughed then pointedly ogled the bruise the raw lighting of the grocery store made visible.

"You'd think this would be the perfect place to care...Since we're all the same here-" the cashier coughed.

The woman looked at the cashier as if she was nothing but a simpering child worth nothing more than disgust. "I'm in a hurry, so... it'd be best if you could speed this up a-"

"Oh! Of course! Wouldn't want anyone to get impatient waiting for your arrival-" the cashier sneered as she dutifully rang up the woman's groceries.

The woman raked her hair back down over the swollen side of her face, ignoring the faint blue bruise where the dysfunctioning Fitbit they'd had to return as it itched, almost seeming to glow.

*

The frazzled, unkempt couple turned further away from the mirror in front of them and one another in the barren, hospital blue, cinder block walled room. Biointellisense monitors were stuck to their foreheads, jugular and various pulse points as they were painstakingly observed through the two way glass.

"It's so odd how humane we find ways to be to the very ones who wanted all of us and our allies exterminated like copulating dogs," the attendant murmured.

"Only to document them turning on each other like animals as soon as all sense of otherness is removed from the equation," remarked their colleague.

"Even solely in their mind's own eye- fascinating, isn't it?" The lead doctor laughed. His attendants blushed over his exuberance.

"Forgive me! I know we've all been through such harrowing times. & I'll be the first to admit it I considered the idea of Racism being a mental illness utter balderdash! But when technology came together and it was actually proven? It was just the breakthrough we needed to discover the penultimate cure-"

"Which turned out to be as old as time, with a lil cybernetic assist: Give the people... what they want... so they can play those parameters all the way out to free themselves from the seduction of it-" the junior

attendant muttered. "Even this current iteration plague is

now almost contained with them under virtual care-"


"The New world is braver than one thought it'd

ever be...To the Fitbit for the foothold in!"

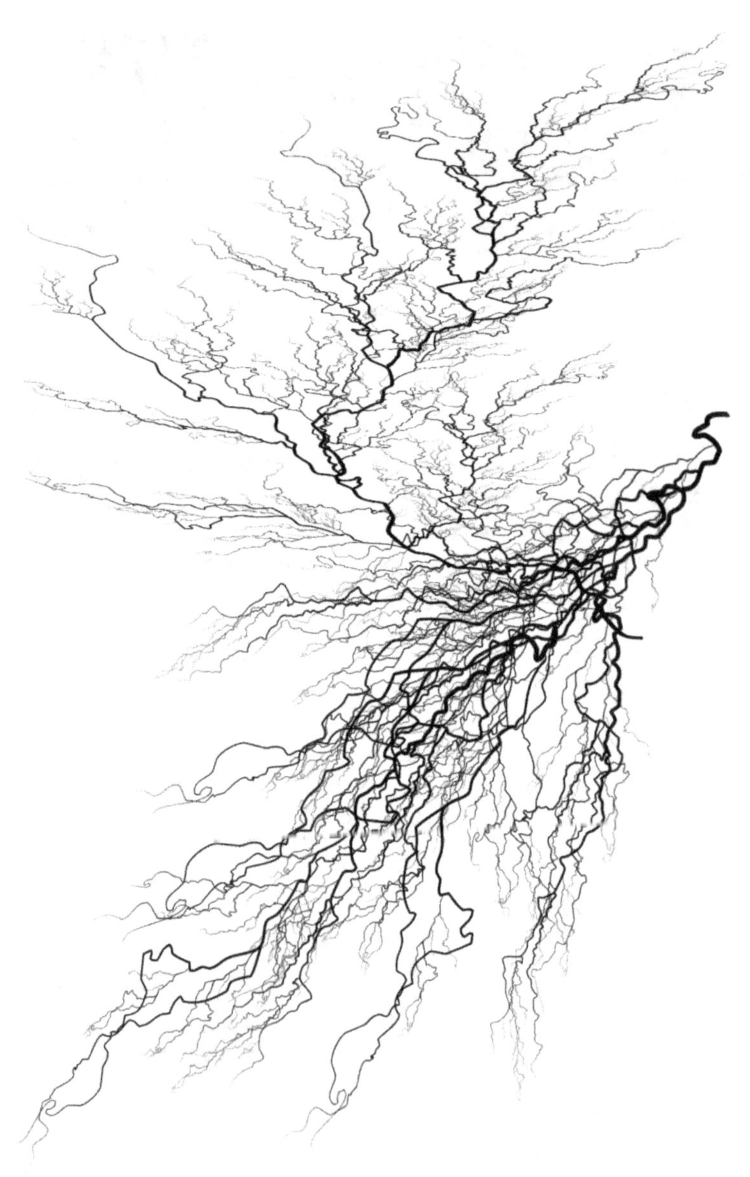

# 16.Third

Chaos comes from the simplest things sometimes.

So many of our greatest minds had prepared for this
moment across genres, space and time.
But none of them hallowed as such had possessed the
clarity of foresight nor the psychological humility the
actuality of such a situation required.

The patriarchal teats they'd been raised on and the societal
proclivities they'd pandered to in order to maintain their
status as illustrious thinkers made thinking outside the
box impossible when it came to the world first finding out
we all were not alone. Officially.

First contact.

Publicized, that is.


Because after the dust cleared as to what exactly went down it also came out that the powers that be had hidden multiple first attempts from everybody on earth, trying to sell us off like bad stock before a market crash, as food or fodder to whichever ones showed up on the scene as the highest bidders.


But no one was buying.

It had never crossed their minds to consider aliens would give no fucks for the psychotic, co-dependent beats we'd all been programmed to dance to, especially those at the top. The sellers were seen as the filmy filth rising to the surface of waters that were suffocating, algae killing a lake. But the aliens said nothing.

...Beyond "no thanks. "

That denial was referenced as the first repulsion by the ones who came.

Insulted at being rebuffed sans rebuke, those who were of the virulent colonizer seed that had wreaked havoc on our planet to stockpile neverending resources and create a semblance of scarcity initiated what we survivors now refer to as the Second contact. Or Second coming. Depends on the camp you're in.

Those declaring themselves to be driving the third planet forward demanded governments attack en masse in the sky what they couldn't comprehend not wanting to eat or enslave us as they had for so long...or be destroyed by the stronger countries around them for refusing to participate in the onslaught.

They were vaporized.

Those..."at the wheel."

Instantaneously.

Damn near rapturously.

Citizens that had been primed as such fell to their knees and screamed... until they nervously realized they could stand up.

With the others.

Like us.

Denizens that gleamed like oil slicks as the aliens did in the dark. Whose hair levitated like theirs. And whose eyes already glowed in the dark.

Because they'd been fucking with the feed for years, the Vaporized. Trying to water it down. Our planetary birthright. Rising up. Calling us to.

Those who'd arrived knew the superheroes were already awakening here.

"We heard it shift in your songs. The vibration. Knew enough was enough," they'd said.

That it was time to come home. Or go.

Offer both to us all. And let which ever one each of us devised in our heart to do be followed.

There were still Beta-minded broods among us who read the vacuum created by the vaporization as wrong as utterly possible.

The peace pissed them off.

So they bided their time, breathless for the chance to ascend like they'd always wanted to and had solely hung around being abused by those in power for all those years, inebriated by proximity to power and pushing through pain, complicit in every aspect of man's inhumanity to man manifesting across the decades before the First and Second coming.

When they saw their chances to usurp latter vestiges of power they took them in spurts, too enamored with the system they'd pledged allegiance to for any ability to process said system being in ruins on its back begging for death to register as they climbed through the fires to the top.

We let them get there.

Time and time again.

Bided ours.

It was through and on them that we found out we could
vaporize too.

I still remember the smell.

Of the spits.

The fields.

We dragged them to.

Of our own instinct and accord.

Tied them to the land the way so many of them had
spilled our blood across generations to earth that was as
foreign beneath their feet as the land had once been to
ours.

Fields of spits. Roasting.

Outside of each town.

That we turned them on.

In clusters.

Systematically shut them down. Not to eat. We just watched as the clarified atmosphere turned them to ash. At our command.

Blessed them as they burned up in their own anger, mixed their purified ash into the earth they'd called cursed due to all the rage they'd held onto over the years they'd not been allowed to Lord over us as masters. They'd never forgiven anyone who had found a semblance of self outside of service.

We learned quickly.

In growing cycles.

Watched the land restore itself in the aftermath of their

false flag attacks against everyone, trying to turn us against those who wouldn't buy us ahead of time. But we knew their marks. They were still our worst beast.

That was the sick beauty of it. Blessing them as they burned canceled out the curses lobbed collectively across time as they strung us from trees like flags of fury they'd forgotten in blazes of fear of aliens.

They blocked out all the violence they'd wrought across color lines, a line that was a figment of their imaginations all along in the sky.

They had lived detached from all our allies that looked like them that they'd massacred trying to slow the shift down.

But the earth hadn't forgotten. Earth never does. She simply welcomed her wayward sons home as dust to start the cycle again.

I was young then.

It was before I chose to be one of the ones to "go," when

curiosity couldn't let me be comfortable with the sweet

smell of hops and human remains that hung in the air

here anymore.

I'm older now.

And on my way back.

To see what I need to see.


I've been warned.

But I'm ready.

We land in T-minus thirteen.

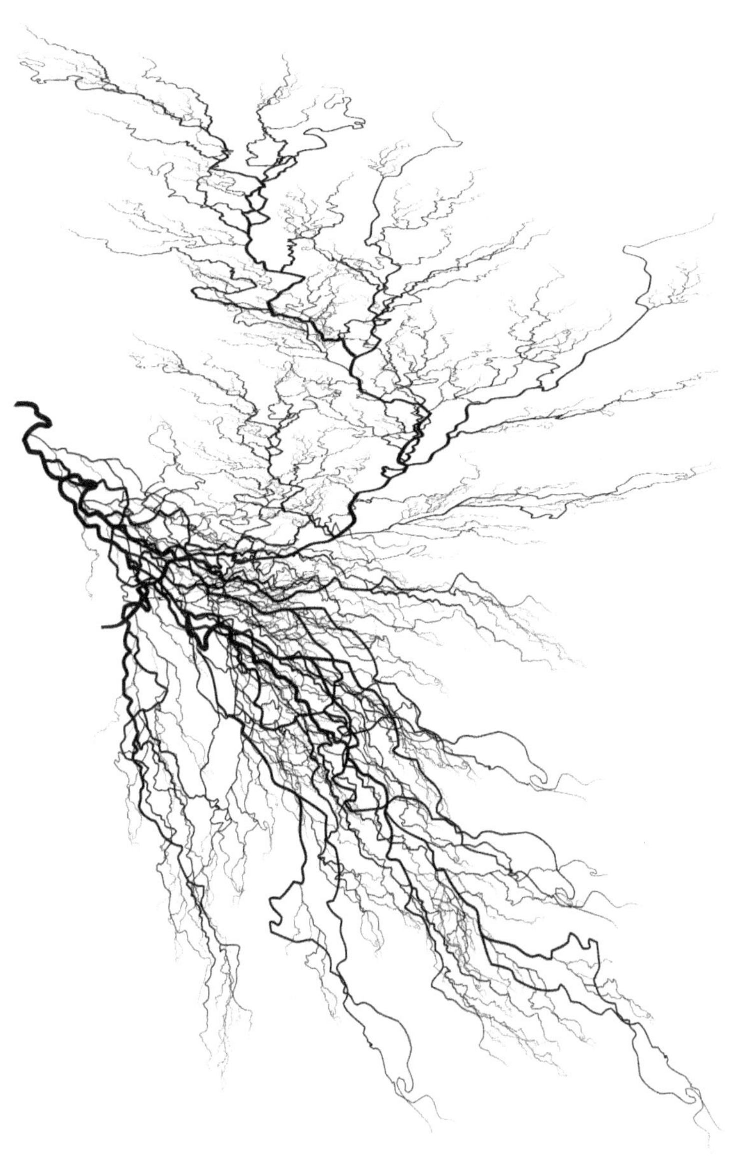

Additional artwork credit:kjpargeter

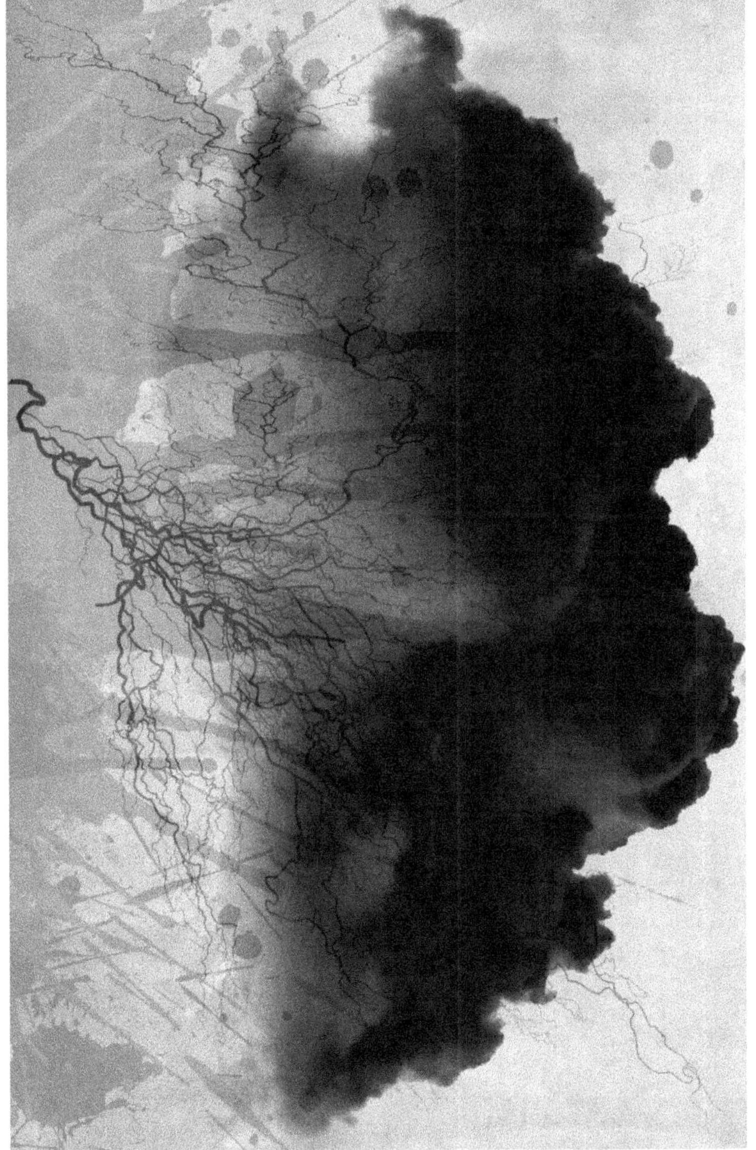

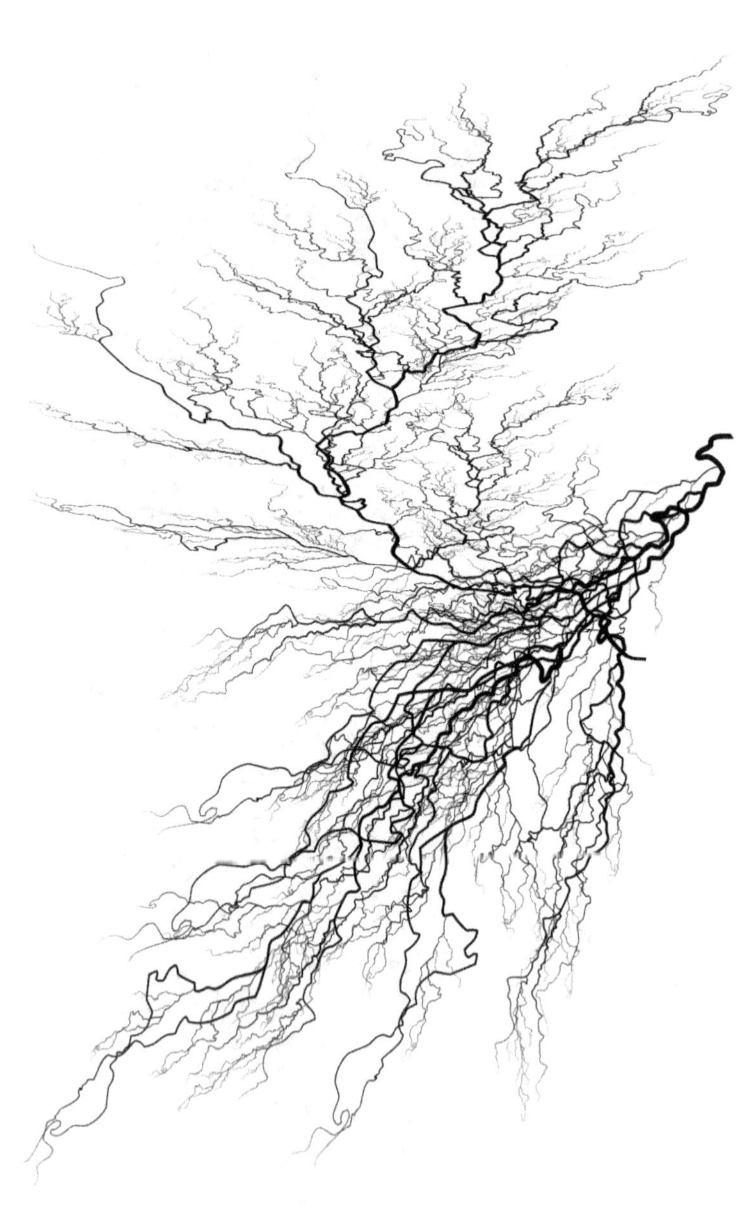

# 17.Veil

His hands shook in his lap.

They had all year.


He did his best to keep his composure as some of them huddled in corners and stared blankly out into the place they used to be able to center themselves in. Others frantically paced around, stepping over still more who were sprawled limply on the floor waiting for prescriptions to kick in.


"They'd been the steadiest out of them all," he thought to himself. "Now look at them."

He felt eyes on him and looked up. His colleague smiled ruefully. "Intubation shakes?"

He nodded. His jaw stiffened. "It's... the pit- " he said, " I just can't any-"

"Maybe you should tap out for the next round-" the other respiratory doctor began to whisper but was cut off.

"We Still don't know what this is- and now they want to use US as guinea pigs for this rushed bullshit?! This is our fucking reward for manning the gap They left?"

He hissed as his anger outran the air in his lungs. "They wont even show them what happens- what we fight here! Even though to SEE it- to fucking See this Hellish abyss firsthand would ensure they'd stay their asses at home! They're hyping them up to kill us all with their fucking stupidity, just to sell new phones Nobody's even going to be around to fucking Use in six months if we don't get a-"

He tried to stop but couldn't. "And my wife, my two girls- they're so scared-I haven't held my two year old in 8 months because I don't want to Kill her-I just- can't even- and now they want to Mandate WE take it first?!- Then who's going to do this?! Them?! THEIR selfish asses?! They're trying to kill us all for trying to Save them! When will it fucking End?!- You know what? FUCK Them!! They don't appreciate Anything!" he roared and convulsed sharply in his hard, plastic chair.

"I can't sacrifice myself anymore for idiots who won't sacrifice hanging out having fucking brunch anymore! I'm not doing this anymore! I'm going ... home-"

The respiratory doctor roughly stood up and remembered

he couldn't go home. Only to that hotel. He looked around and saw the stricken faces of his colleagues all witnessing him fall apart.

But what he initially read as horror he instantly understood was pure, also overwhelmed compassion.

A spasm of shame shot across his shoulders and finally released as he broke, chin slammed to chest as he crumpled back down into his seat, tears he'd held back for so long soaking the thighs of his khakis.

He wailed.
In front of them all.

The way they all had eventually done.

He'd been the last one standing.

Watching him cry out tore something deep within everyone present and they all began to softly break, sobbing together in solidarity against nightmares no one else was going to have to understand because of the thankless sacrifices they kept making.

*

"I think they've had enough-" a faceless man muttered to the one beside him on the other side of the looking glass.

"It says here we have to wait until at least one of them has harmed-"

"They've HAD...Enough," he growled aggressively. The one beside him stepped back nervously.

"Yes Sir-" He looked over his shoulder and gave the nod.

The lights flickered overhead in the doctor's lounge. Those inside of it knocked into each other and crashed onto the carpeted floor like slapped down dominoes.

The veil shifted and the watchers flooded into the space to inspect the wet, distressed faces of them all before gingerly dancing their hands across the each medical professional, drying tears and spiriting their souls back to the beds they'd left their bodies on to commune with the only ones who could comprehend the war they were in.

And to cry .
With one another.
On the frontlines in dreams the way protocol would never allow in real time,

In hopes of baptizing the space ahead of the next shifts,

giving some semblance of Holiness in the midst of Hell.

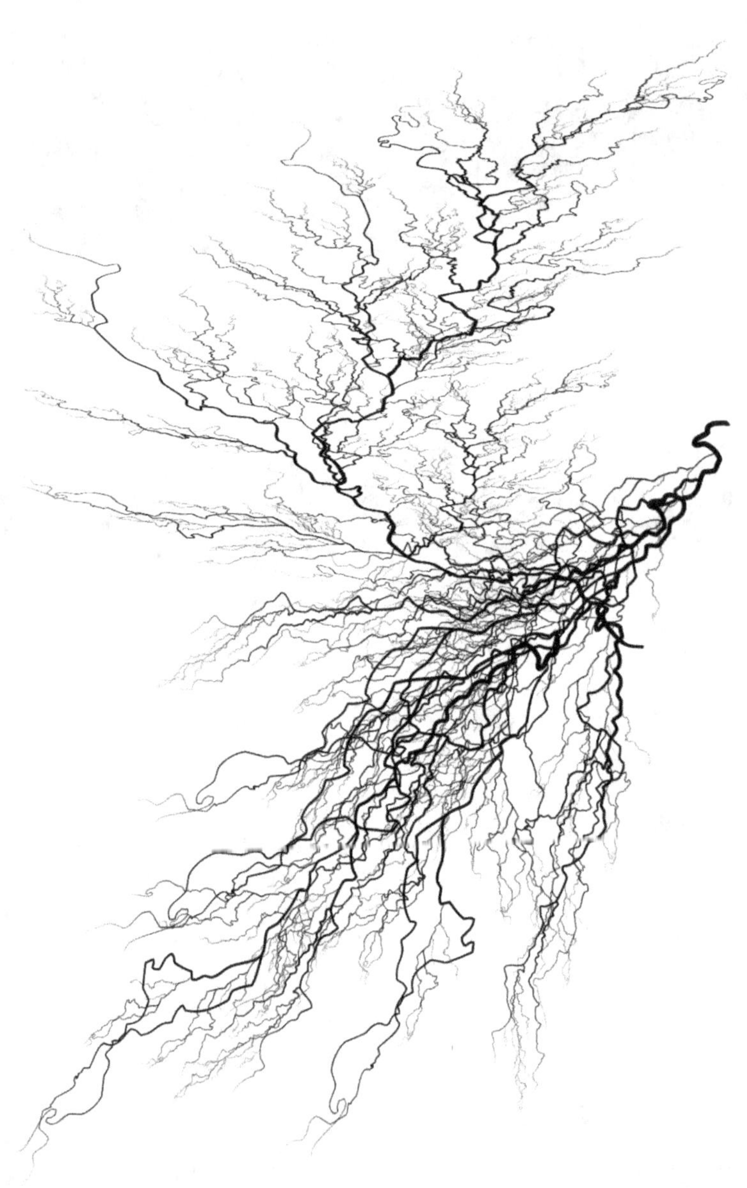

# 18. Koshima.

"You either want it or you don't. You can't claim to want it for you & then hate other manifestations of it for others and expect that to bother coming into your life- it has to feel welcomed in every-" the old man muttered.

"It's not the same," he started to protest but his elder cut him off.

"Sure it is! Everything you sit up here and complain about, everything I hear you make fun of your sisters for, everything I have watched you obsess over your whole dang life- it's all dancing around one thing and one thing only-"

"Would you gentlemen like a refill?"

The waitress with the tightest rollerset on Tuesdays drawled in a laidback way that matched the relaxation of her curls to her favorite Friday afternoon customers.

"No maam, thank you-" the flustered man murmured to the woman who'd been his coming of age crush what felt like millennia ago. The smirk on his grandfather's face turned the tops of his already blushing ears bright red.

"Betty, Baby. It's Elisabeth... you're grown up enough to call me that now," she grinned. His grandpa chuckled.

"No, no thank you...Betty!"he croaked like his voice was changing all over again.

"Just as cute as ever," she laughed and asked the old man who sat in her section everyday with one of his kids or grandchildren in the diner if he was good.

Betty winked at the man as she turned to leave. Grandpa let out a low whistle as the man sat there gape mouthed in shock, swiveling his neck to watch her go.

"I told you, word...has...spread~" his grandfather sang. His grandson blushed, then burst out laughing.

He'd needed it. Every part of it.
"Telling you granddaddy, these Friday mornings with you have been like water for a man stumbling through the desert-"

His grandfather's face softened. He hadn't called him granddaddy since he'd been seven years old. "I feel the same way about you, boy- but look... you gotta get your head around this. You can't hate & love it at the same time and think it's going to see you as home. Not in there. Pick a side, man. It's never once & for all. You can always change your choice down the road. But choose it all the way, man!...it has to feel... it's going to be honored by you 100%... "

The sunlight in the old diner shifted in a way that told them their time was up.
He pulled out his billfold to pay, then tossed a bit extra on the table. The man started to do the same but his grandfather stopped him. The grandson looked beseechingly at him.

The old man then followed his eyes to the woman of his boyhood dreams. He pulled his hand back as his grandson tucked every bill he'd had but one under his cleaned plate so she'd know it was from him.

They both stood up and walked to the door. The old man tipped his hat at Elisabeth as per norm. She curtsied like she always playfully did.

"They've gotten really good with this thing, haven't they?" the man murmured.

"More like I remember, every time. What about her?" the old man grinned knowingly.

"Even more beautiful than I recalled her, which I wouldn't have ever thought was possible," the man whispered, looking over his shoulder as they crossed the threshold. "Thanks for that. For her, for- I mean-" he stopped short of stammering as he leaned in for a goodbye hug.

"Had a feeling she'd help, " the old man laughed. "Besides, you deserve someone who makes you laugh and live, not cry- a chick who makes your ears hot!"

"Thanks granddaddy," he whispered. "Bye?"

"I'm ready when you are," the old man chuckled as they held onto each other as they roughly exploded into a shower of synaptic sparks somewhere out in the infinite folds of the space-time continuum.

*

The man woke up gently, sweet smile on his face, Our-Tyme nodules still blinking on his temples, the only light besides him in the dreary unkempt bachelor's apartment.

Gingerly placing them in their compartment on the nightstand, he sat up, swung his feet out and hoisted himself all the way out of bed for the first time in forever.

He winced through his first steps, pushing himself towards the curtains to open them for the first time.

The attendants looked at him cautiously when they saw he was smiling.

He gave the thumbs up sign.

They cheered on the other side of the glass as all the airlocks and deadbolts to the containment room opened.

He collapsed in shock after his first draught of actual air but came too quickly enough, utterly healed of despair and depression.

He was their 100th patient. To survive without going insane. He had died trapped in the nightmarish confines of his own mind. And had been revived twelve times before he'd learned to navigate the worm-holing apparatus dreams, thought and memory shared that science had discovered and business was now racing to profit off of.


It was ready for the market.

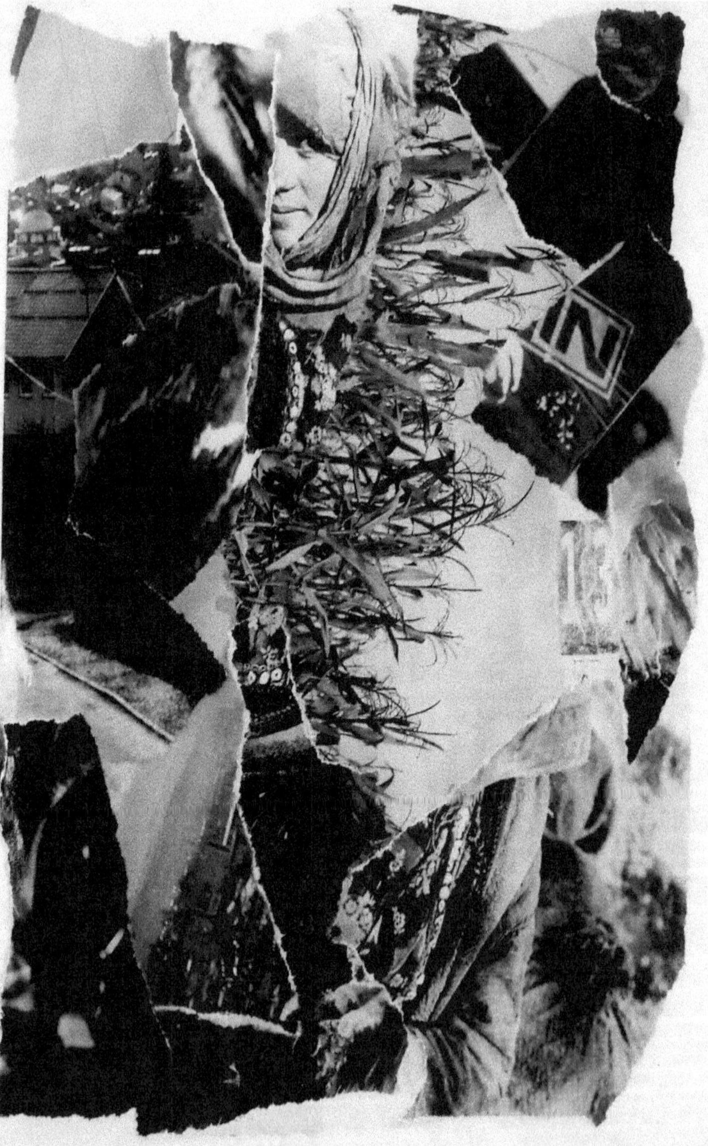

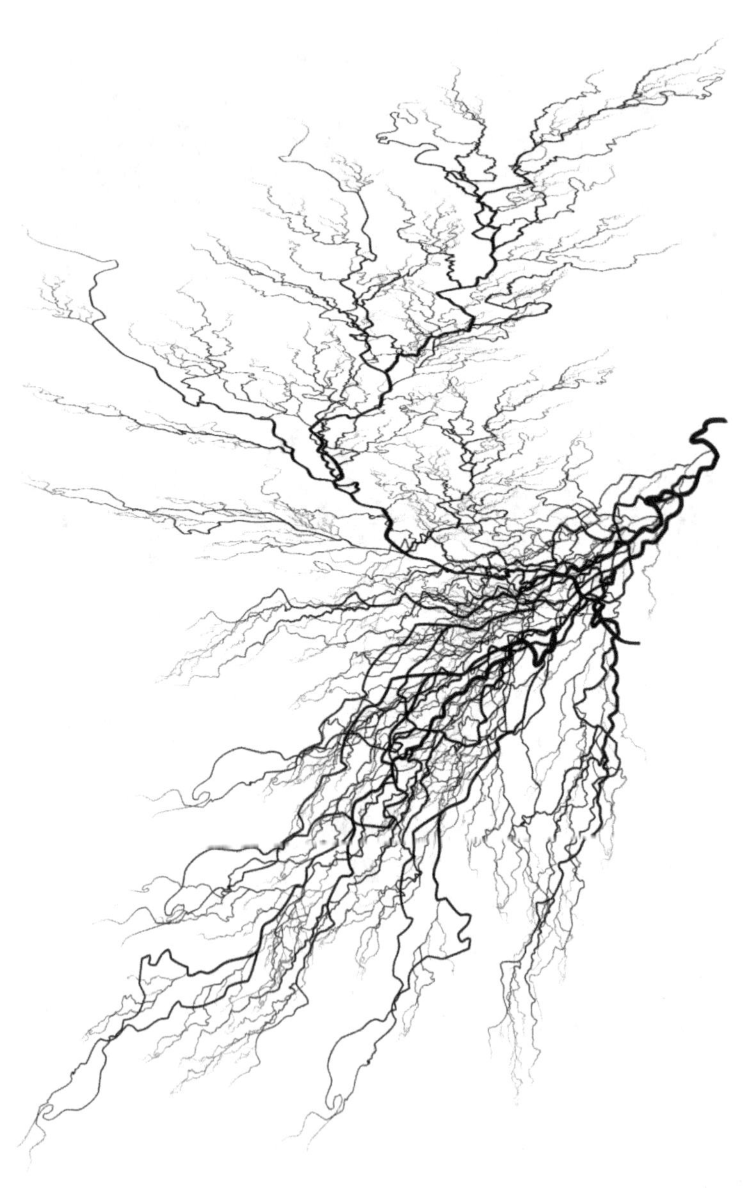

# 19. Process.

"Mamba honey, just open it!"

" ...that's what I'm trying to do!"she yelled.

It was getting worse. All of it. But whether they came to terms with it in time or not everyone was having to –

"Just figure it the Fuck out! Or let me help!"she roared at her friend. Silky bottle blond hair danced down her shoulders like a buttery slip, hiding her hunched over molting back until she abruptly stood up.

"You can't help me with this and you fucking know it!"she screamed, ran out the room and defiantly flung herself into the driver's side of the car.

Anemone massaged the bony protrusion now in the center of her brow bone a bit ruefully, finally realizing what it was she was feeling.

Gratitude.

She was grateful that the off center lil horn had been the end of it for her after the scattering of teeny feathers beneath her shoulder blades. Narwhals were her favorite and she'd always felt like the girl in the last unicorn growing up as it was.

And her dude? He'd always been a full on guardian angel to her anyway so the strange black feathers that had shot out from his armpits and had meandered down his most ticklish places on the inside of his upper limbs were a relief but not a surprise.

But all around them there had been many horrific ones.

"You don't have to go get in that car with her." he murmured from his perch on the couch.

"You know that I do." Anemone hissed.

"Just," he paused, weighing his words, "be careful-"
She rolled her eyes "You never liked her!"she snapped and turned around to face him.

"Yeah, & there's a reason for that!"he laughed as he stood up and squared off with her in the way that always made her smile. She looked away, fighting off both the charm and the sincerity he was hitting her with. "Look- alls I'm saying is... these times? We never know what we're gonna get. Except in the cases that we do. Look at me?"

She looked at him as he gently grazed her red ochre hued cheek. "I know... she likes you. But... I also know how I've seen her treat others that could be related to you when you aren't around. She may be better than I have the ability to see her as, she may be worse. But my opinions are moot in this. We're all about to have to deal with what actually IS regardless of what it feels better to think, including her. So... if you're going to ride along...be prepared to fly if you have to. Remember Laith."

"It happened right before my eyes. " Anemone whispered, still shook. "Maybe it's not today! Maybe the count is off-"

Urchin wrapped his arms around Anemone. "Well... that'd explain why she couldn't but.... then it'd be tomorrow . Go lay down. I'll handle it."

The memory of Laith had her so aghast that she docilely did as told, hearing the screen door latch behind Urchin as he went out to the drive.

*

Mamba was so absorbed in the light playing across the water droplets on the windshield that she jumped when Urchin knocked on the window. She rolled it down, no love lost between the two of them.

"Where is she?"she asked flatly.

"Having a flashback to what happened with Laith." Urchin said as plainly.

Mamba winced.

"Look! It's not like I-" Mamba began defensively. "I'm nothing like-"

"You're nothing like the guy you spent all of your free time with when you weren't with Anemone for how many years?-" Urchin deadpanned.

"Just because he was that way – he turned out to be a fucking snake of a racist asshole doesn't mean I am like him!" Mamba cried out.

"You're right, Mamba. Him being a venomous piece of racist shit doesn't mean you are. That you never called him on it does." Urchin growled.

Mamba started to cry. "I'm not an asshole! I'm not a- look at all the good I do for that community-" she bawled. "I do a lot of good in the world – I'm not like those selfish assholes! I care! And who are you to attack me?! How dare you accuse me of being whatever you're trying to accuse me of?! I'm not like him, you... whatever you are now!"

"Oh, I know. " Urchin growled menacingly. Mamba's crocodile tears dried up apprehensively as the last hairs on the back of her neck stood up and fell off quietly onto her shoulders.

"I just came out here and told you your best friend -who you knew hadn't slept all week- had been triggered by your erratic turning behavior into reliving Laith's Meta attack...and it didn't even cross your fucking mind to get out of your fucking car to go see about your fucking friend. You just sat here crying over yourself." Urchin hissed, " I already know exactly what the fuck you are. It's not going to be a big reveal at all. But she loves you. Which means there's fucking hope. But it's gonna be up to you what you fucking turn into... and you're not taking her with you either way. I slit Laith's throat in self defense protecting her but it'd be fucking premeditated with you. Meta or not. Fucking Try me, Mamba."

Mamba's ashen skin began to glisten in strange patches across her face as her beady eyes went red. "You can't talk to me like that! – I'll-" Mamba raged.

"You'll what? Call them? A mid Meta calling them to try to get me killed?" Urchin laughed. "See, that's part of your kinds problem. Cognitive dissonance over what has finally changed. Who...do you think... they'll shoot first now, with all your molting symptoms and frantic behavior? You really think they're gonna aim at me? Or worse, her because of the color of her skin? Soon as they see these wings or that horn... all guns you called will point to your vindictive, passive aggressive, racist, blanched ass."

She opened a mouth the man who'd just threatened her knew contained nothing but death... but no sound came out.

"No? Good...now get the fuck out of my driveway and Meta your damned self. Prove me wrong, Mamba. Because if you prove me right it won't matter what you shift into. " Urchin hissed."You come for her with your racist shit unleashed and I'll end you."

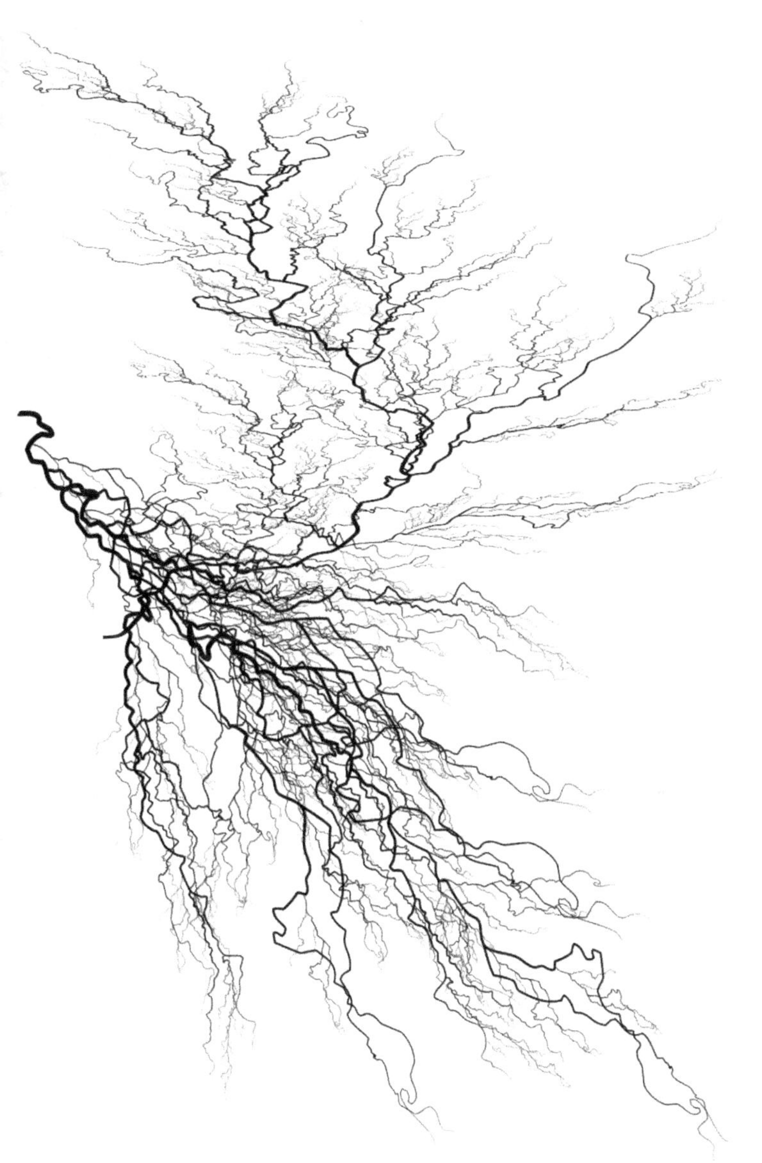

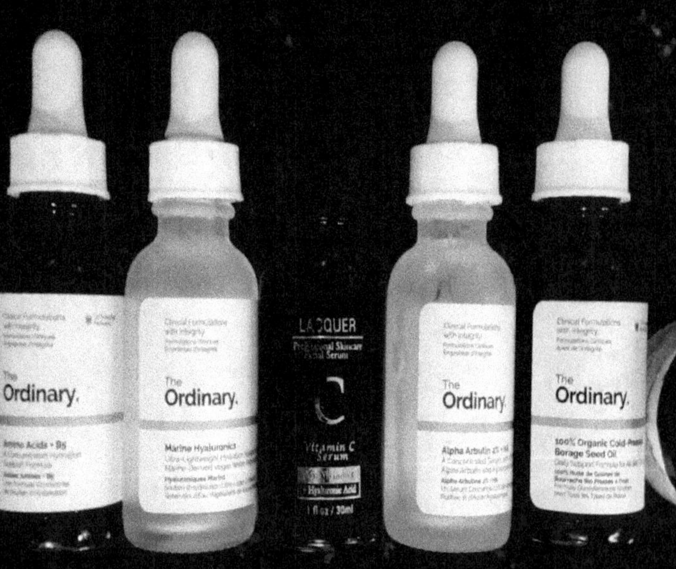

DKNY

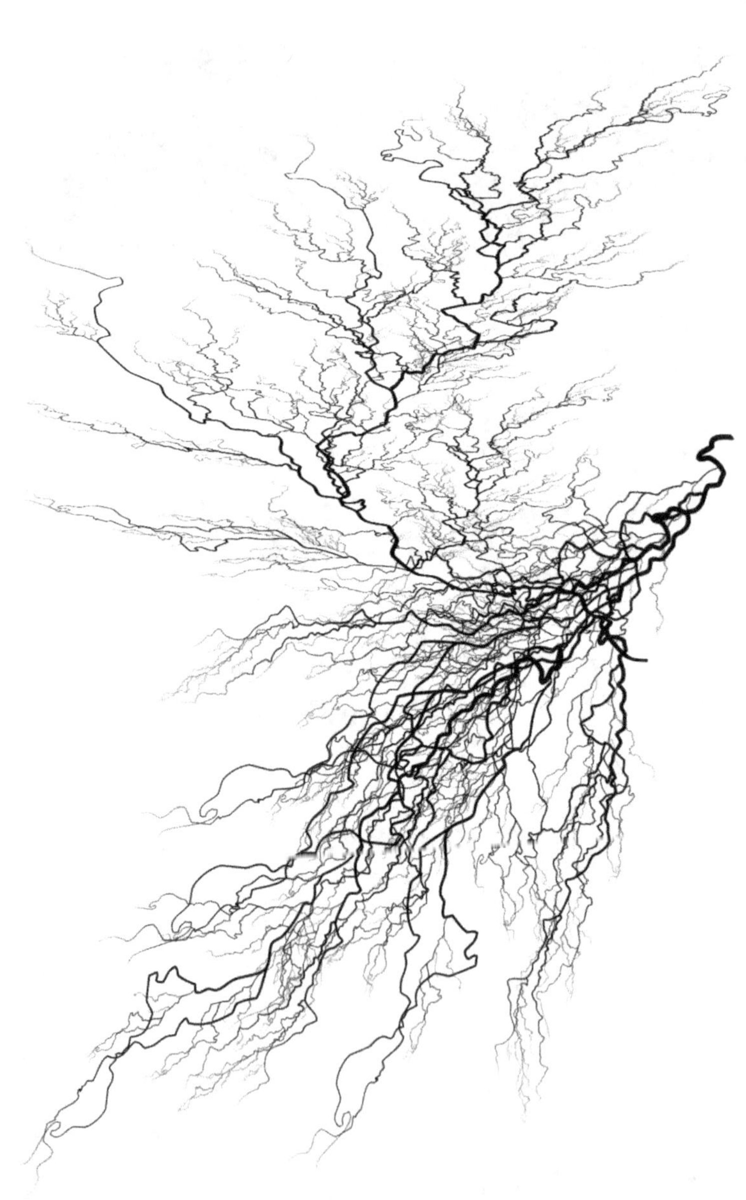

# 20. ministry

The baby screamed like it was about to explode.


Again.


Another one.


The harried look on the mother's face told everyone around her all they needed to know except for one person.

"It's still not time-" the doctor said ambivalently.

"Doctor, you can't be serious!" the attendants present argued.

"They can't be in that much pain, neither of them, it's impossible, nothing more than theatrics, " he said with a wave of his hand.

The baby roared on the other side of the glass, shaking it. The mother swooned as she held onto her child for dear life.

"That's IT!" the second attendant screamed as he lunged for the doctor and knocked his clipboard to the floor. The doctor leaped back in shock.

"We have LOST thirteen mothers due to your fucking inability to conceive of anything that looks like them as capable of experiencing anything akin to pain!"
"YOU don't get to speak to Me that-" the doctor snarled as the attendant tackled him to the waxed linoleum floor and wrapped his fingers around his throat.

Marta said his name softly, as if they were all in a dream.
"Harry,"

"Yes, Marta?" he said calmly, not looking back at her.


"Marta! MARTA!" the doctor screamed, "Get him off of me! Use the scalpel to your-" the doctor was slick with fear for the first time in ages.

"Tell-t -tell me to administer the sugar, Harry-" James stammered softly.

"Go administer the sugar, James," Harry muttered as he dug the bony tips of his fingers into the malignant doctor's voice box.


James scurried off as the doctor screamed for Marta to save him. "The scalpel! Marta, do it! You're like one of us, almost- you know where to cut!"

"You've transcended the threshold of death you littered with their bodies for so long-" Harry barked.

"No. Matter. What. Happens. Next. Your . Time. Here. Is. Done!" The doctor snarled, straining to look away from his slowly blue turning face in the dirty lenses of Harry's glasses.

The idea of Marta violently stabbing Harry to save the Doctor aroused the same stiffness in his loins that his experiments had set his crotch aflame with every single time. He licked his blue lips to regroup, straining against the weight of Harry choking him. It was his first time tasting his own medicine.

"You should've made the right call, Doc. You always made the wrong call-" Harry muttered.

Suddenly the screams of the baby stopped, filling the doctor with outrage at the possibility of it being comforted by droplets he didn't sanction.

"Kill this beast of- Marta! MARTA!!Now, dammit! You slow, passive idiot! Can't you hear me?!"

Vitriol spewed out of the doctor, the closest he was going to get to the bloom of adrenaline in himself that he'd tormented so many things once temporarily labeled women and children past the brink of in the name of science.

Decades misconstruing their sudden peace over twisted death by his hands as the expression of some genetically based supernatural ability to be isolated disintegrated as he understood against his will that it was a natural reaction of all beings to the absurdity and actuality of the futility of fighting against fate. He realized in that moment that these were his last.

"You went from murdering them all to orphaning the- just to carve the small ones up, keeping them on support-" Harry whispered harshly. "...you always made the wrong call-"

"He's going -to- to Kill me!" The doctor screamed hoarsely. He soiled himself then burst into tears as he saw Marta finally grab the scalpel out of the corner of his bulging eyeball and bloom over Harry's right shoulder.

"Harry,"
The smell of shit bloomed every time the doctor squirmed between Harry's heavy legs.
"Harry-"

Marta whispered his name like it was the only name that had brought her any peace in this godforsaken place called the Ministry of Life, a dead zone that trafficked in nothing but blood due to the doctors helming the ship towards a purged future no one could see in this hell.

"Yes, Mar?" Harry whispered as he closed his eyes, knowing the protocols that had been programmed into her forever.

"…move, Harry~" she murmured.
Eyes still closed, Harry let go of the doctor's neck and collapsed in a heap off to the side.

The doctor yelped with relief and tried to frantically kick away from where he'd defecated as Marta offered her hand to him.

"That-!"he gasped, "What took you so long?! That animal was go-going to kill me!" the doctor fussed as he wobbled trying to stand.

He slipped in his own shit and roughly grabbed onto Marta's scrubs, exposing the jagged scar that all the corpses of the mothers he'd murdered were tagged with.

"That beast of burden was going to Kill Me! He was going to Kill-" the doctor froze mid-sentence as his eyes landed on some of his earliest handiwork, "M-me-" he stammered.

"No he wasn't," Marta said softly as she stepped around him, slashing his throat wide open as she did.
He dropped to his knees drenched with his own blood.

His neck gaped like a fish gasping for air on the shore as he ogled her scar in disbelief. She followed his eyes & laughed softly.

"Ah...From before you were allowed to kill us to harvest the supposed immortal cells you found, or enslave us to harvest as a supplement to your medicines. Time flies," she shrugged. "Your kind was too arrogant to bother to check records you didn't keep against things you all would never admit to having done, " she added. "You okay, baby?"

"Yes, momma," Harry hiccuped.
"Go prepare the table, Harry."
"Okay momma." Harry said stiffly and did as he was told. He lumbered into the viewing room and watched the sugar water rain onto the belly of the mother James had saved in a daze.

"Did you put everything back into her in the right order?"
Harry asked him.

"I-I think, I think so, yeah, " James said softly, becoming a
bit more confident and steady as he did. " I think I put it
all back in correctly."


Right beside the mother's texturized head, droplet after
droplet splashed gently onto the newborn's chest, slowly
slid around him then soaked in. Once he was saturated
with peace the synthetic amniotic fluid would self stitch a
protective sac around the baby, allowing it to grow to term
outside the womb, magnificent technology that had been
rejected due to its efficacy supporting the very segments
of society that the Doctor's kind had gone infertile
themselves trying to eradicate.

It had been relegated to use in the genomic farms the prized and pristine Ministries of Life once were to stretch out the feed of the supplemental slaughterhouses that originally harvested human growth hormone they'd become when tastes changed.

Now it was only used in to keep alive specimens between rounds of disjointed experimentation meant to extend the shelf life of the produced product.

Viewing rooms no one entered any longer due to the decimation wrought on the already impotent ranks of those like the Doctor by the wasting sickness the cannibalism triggered across the population via the slow supplementation of the ministry's products were coated with thick layers of dust.

Those who did the mental gymnastics necessary to doubt the once agreed upon humanity of their targets due to the corrosive hunger that had exploded upon in their brains upon the third feeding devoured one another once in full bloom.

In corroded, half empty regional towers surrounded by the rubble and detritus trying to kill off the majority had left the remnants of society trapped within in lieu of promised land lives, most of the staff operated on autopilot.

Until today .

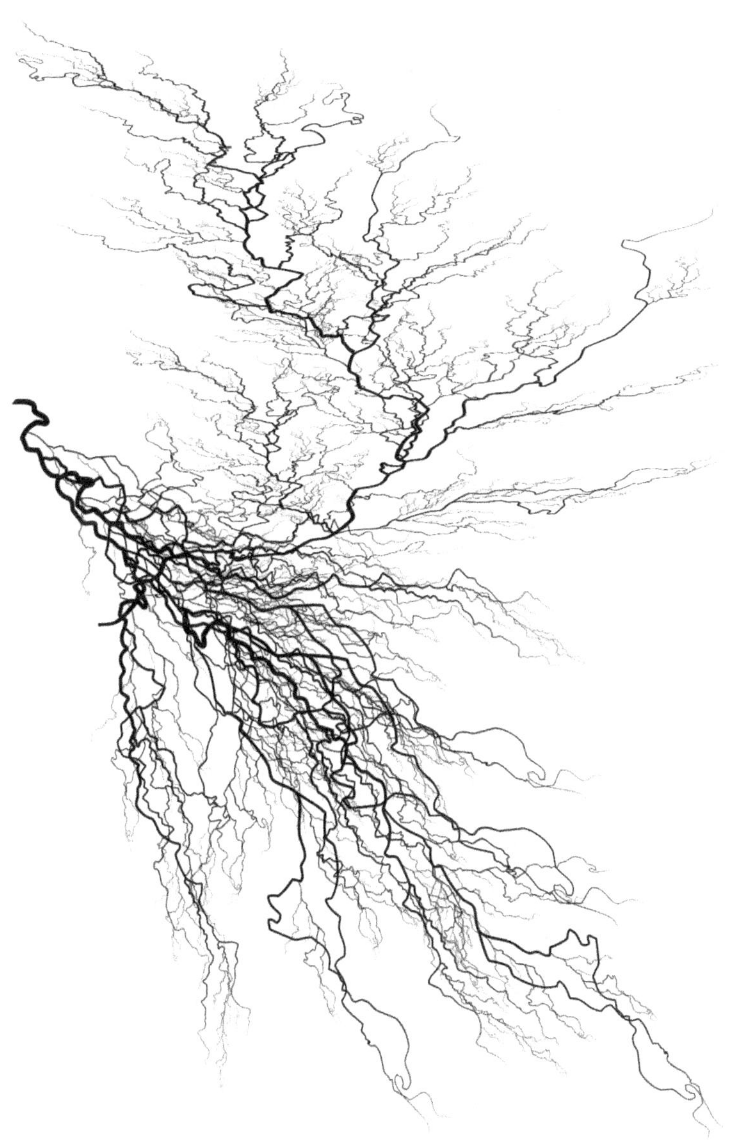

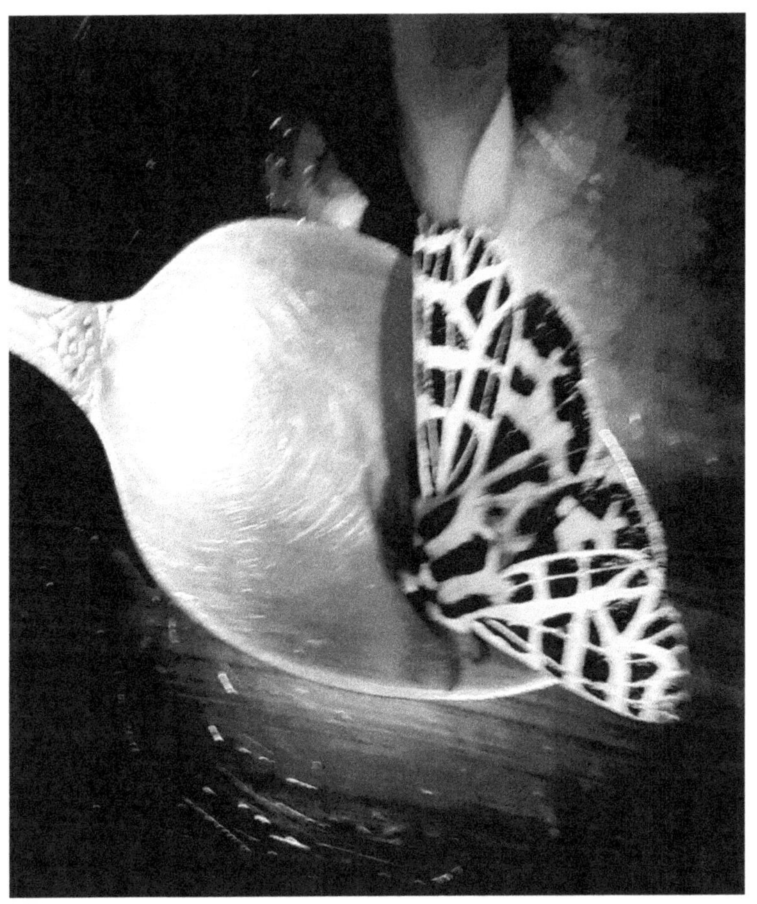

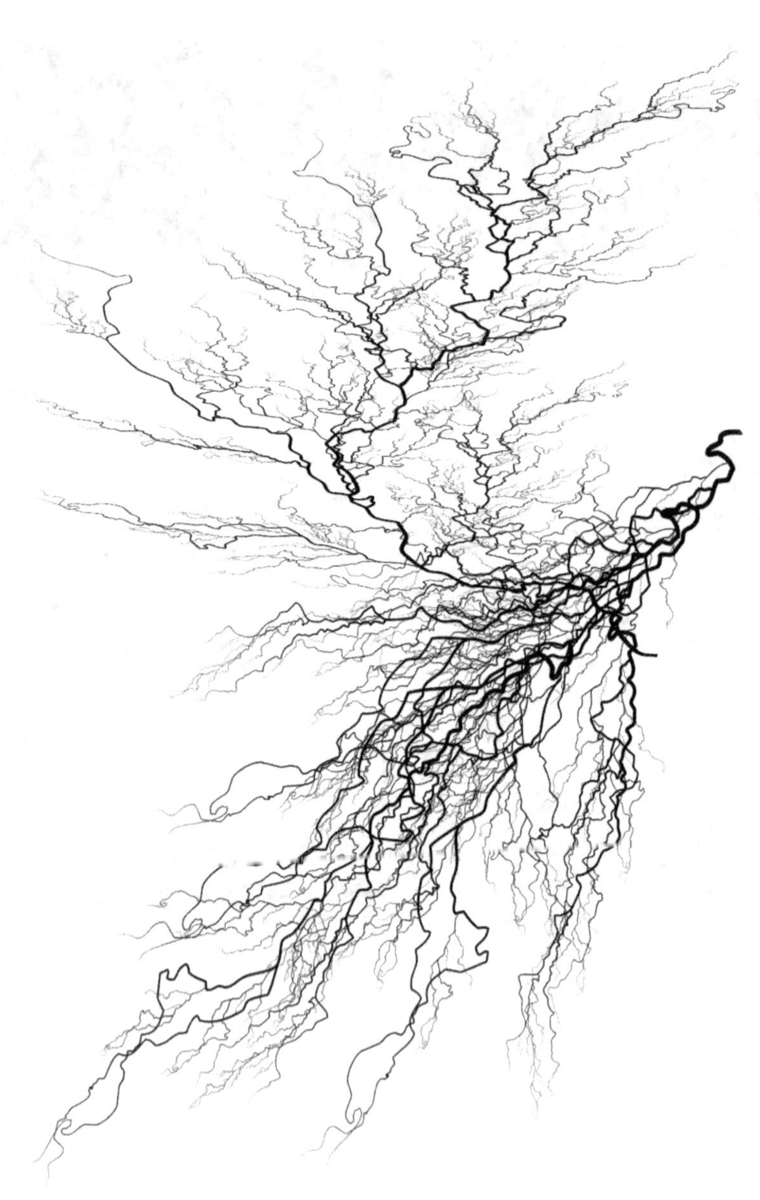

# 21. Flatline

Epiphany stood stock still in the rubble.

Standing in the obvious aftermath of hellish heat made no sense of the wetness that suctioned to every aspect of her or the ash that danced in the heavy air like filthy snow.

She knew she had to.

She took the step.

It started again.

The laughter.

Everything went dark.

*

Against her will her eyes were dragged to the writhing pile of bedding that hovered above the distressed woman across the way as it slowly descended.

The woman's crazed giggles turned to shrieks as the bedding made contact with her flesh & began to violently suffocate the sound out of her. Again.

She knew blinking wouldn't make any of it go away and ripped her eyes up to the ceiling, reminding herself to be grateful that was all she did see.

Epiphany could feel the stricken look beaming out of the one a few meters to her left and absently wondered if the apparitions she was seeing were arms clawing or legs climbing up and down Dee. But not enough to engage.

The last time she had done so was with the one who'd been to her right. The one who'd had no built-in buffer saw gaping mouths devouring the soul of Dee (the distressed one) on a loop for 96 hours straight before she cracked and started yelling out what she saw at the top of her lungs, imploring Ephy to help as everything from her pov dissolved. She'd had to be forcibly removed in the cover of darkness, screaming until she was stopped by what made everyone else there stay inside after dark.

Ephy had heard the sonic shift up in Rolanda's screech as it had echoed out in the badlands that seemed to sprawl out from their place and saturate the clinically pristine neighborhood with dankness, as if whatever had taken her had come from behind and swept her Up as it sunk in to what was left of her.

The tremulous lilt hung in the immediately silent atmosphere like it had been encapsulated in little Epiphany Echt's ear, knowing its end had somehow been witnessed.

A bell chimed.

*

Epiphany gritted her teeth as the apparatuses built into the bed revved up for final procedures.

She slipped her hands willingly into the forearm straps as the automated aspect that cradled her head corrected her posture without warning, pulling her into alignment so the amount of space between each vertebra was to spec and chakras were aligned for the sequential bursts of color-coded light to be administered.

"Fuck!"she grunted as her eyes rolled back in her head and the protective hallucinatory veil began to fade.

Beyond her toes through the fringe of her lowered lashes she watched as the clutch of adrenaline soaked technicians in lab coats and nothing else but body fluid one by one disengaged from Dee's stricken form.

More lab techs rushed in to take the vitals of their blank faced colleagues. One of the dead eyed attendants felt Epiphany's stare and looked over his shoulder at her menacingly.

*



The little girl awoke with a start.
The smell of smoke was everywhere.

Strange light pressed through the horizontal slats in the walls of the tiny dark space she was in and danced across the nail beds of her stiff toes and the knife she'd carried on her since her dad died.

Her back was pressed into the corner at an odd angle and her head hung forward heavily, her own heartbeat lulling her back to sleep. Darkness crashed into her like a wave of icy water and she was out again.

*

Her eyes flipped open.

He was there the way he had been before.

His slackened face glistened in the half light as he stood at the foot of her big sister's bed on the far side of the room the four siblings had shared before Rolanda ran away.

The eldest.

Ephy had been in the closet when their mother had attacked Rolanda for telling on him, detailing what he'd tried to do to her and what she'd then caught the mother's boyfriend doing to Deonne as she slept.

Ephy had been hiding there when Rolanda's body had been found in the field weeks after running away by the neighborhood kids. She had even been there when the mother and him had lied to the police, saying they'd had to put Rolanda out for using drugs and trying to seduce their eventual stepfather for money to buy more.

She had been in there when the mother had screamed at Deonne for finally finding her voice.

"Who is going to pay these bills for this fucking roof over our heads if I make him stop?! & besides no one will believe you if you say a fucking word!"

And Ephy had been in that closet when Dee burned that fucking house to the ground with the mother and that so-called man of hers in it for the whole neighborhood to see.

... but Ephy wasn't in that closet anymore.

*

The inner child looked up in confusion as the knob turned. No one but her and her dad knew about the secret prohibition closet built into the walls of their creaky, old house. "Maybe I'm finally dead... it feels like we've been asleep forever."the lil girl whispered to her shadow.

"Daddy?" Her voice cracked.

"No Ephy, it's...me-I remembered, I remembered where I hid you–" the adult version of herself cried out and ripped the door off its hinges to free her inner child.

Ephy rushed out into the arms of Epiphany, the adult version of herself, craned her face up to look at who she'd become anyway, bewildered.

"You mean we really made it!?" Ephy sobbed.

"...barely, but yeah," Epiphany laughed as her tears rained down on the little kid version of her like rain. "You're going to get another chance to be a kid... with someone watching over you who loves the fuck outta you."

"Who?!" Ephy croaked out,"everybody's gone-"

"I'm gonna be your mother now," she whispered to her smaller self. "I'm going to be the ... you're going to have sooo much fun-"

*

"Should we pull her all the way from up under, Dr. Eudaimon?"

"No... not yet." He whispered softly. "Let them re-engage fully before bringing her back. They have a long road ahead of them. "

"Yes, Doctor. "

Doctor Hugh Eudiamon went back to his office and firmly closed the door.

He leaned against his desk and massaged the cartilage he normally clipped his pince nez to to get his thoughts straight before he began. The heaviness of his work wore gentle furrows in his face but they lit up on days like today, few and far between though they were.

"Logbook-" he called out.
The recording device whirled into action.


"Subject finally didn't flatline upon seeing the knife her father had used to disembowel himself due to shame over his wife's transgressions- the Lost has indeed finally been found. "

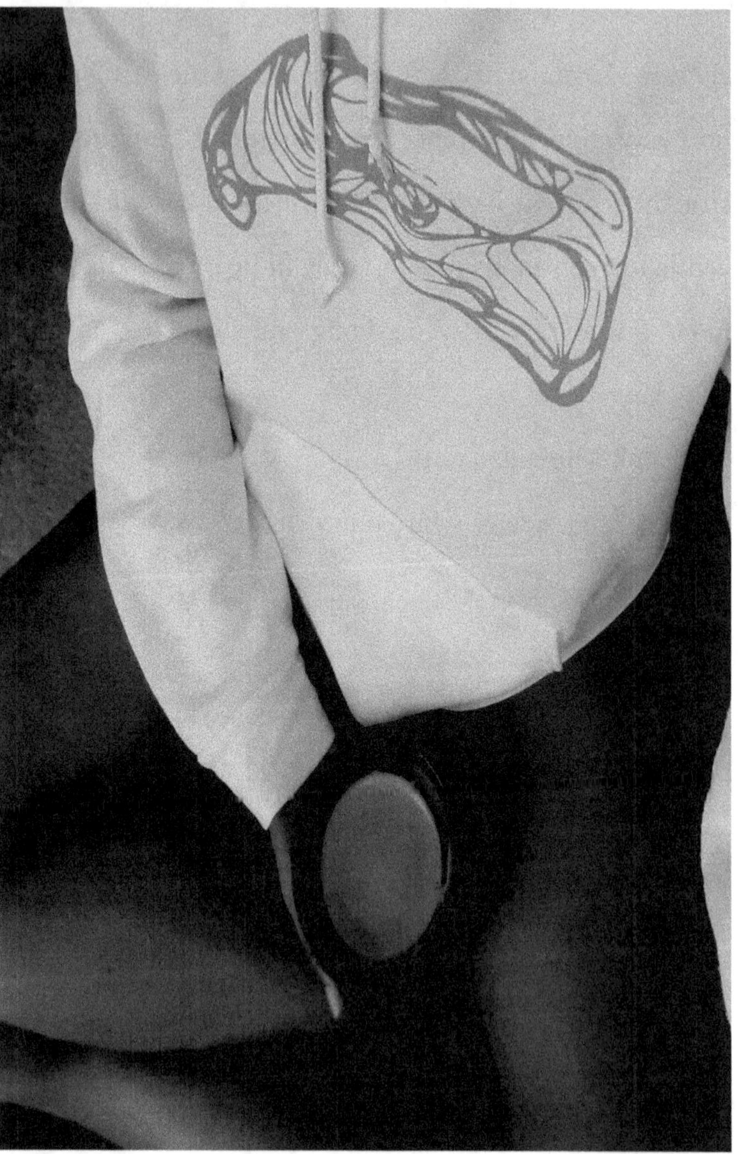

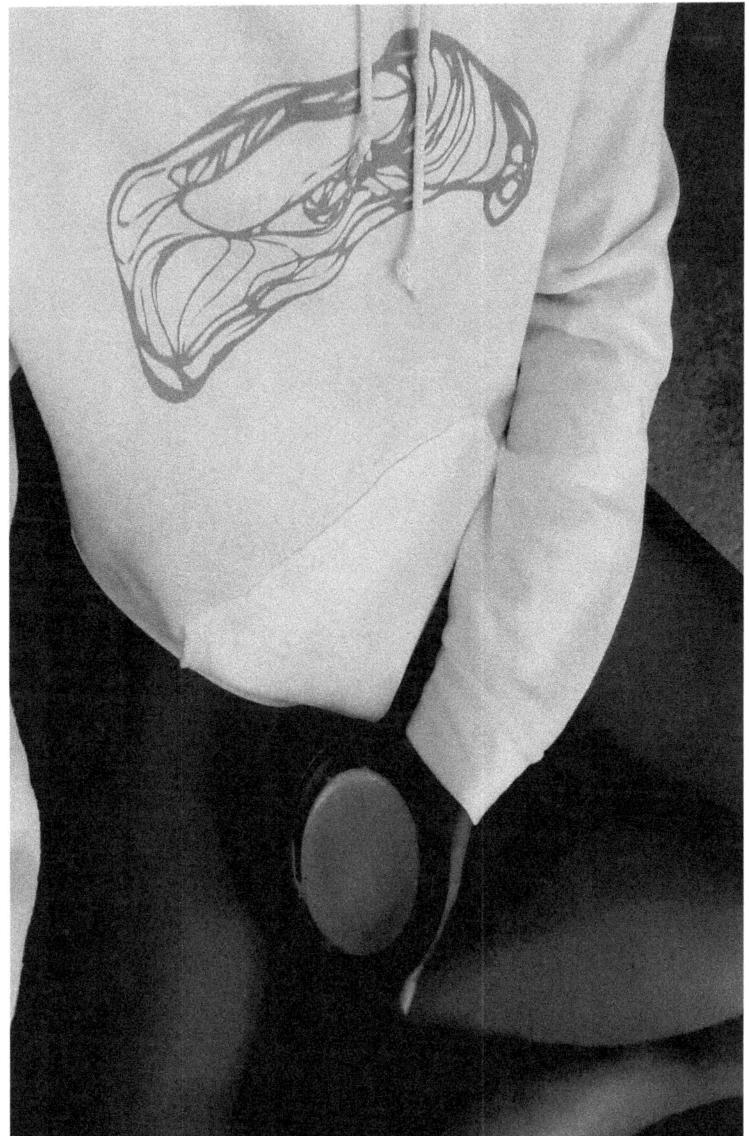

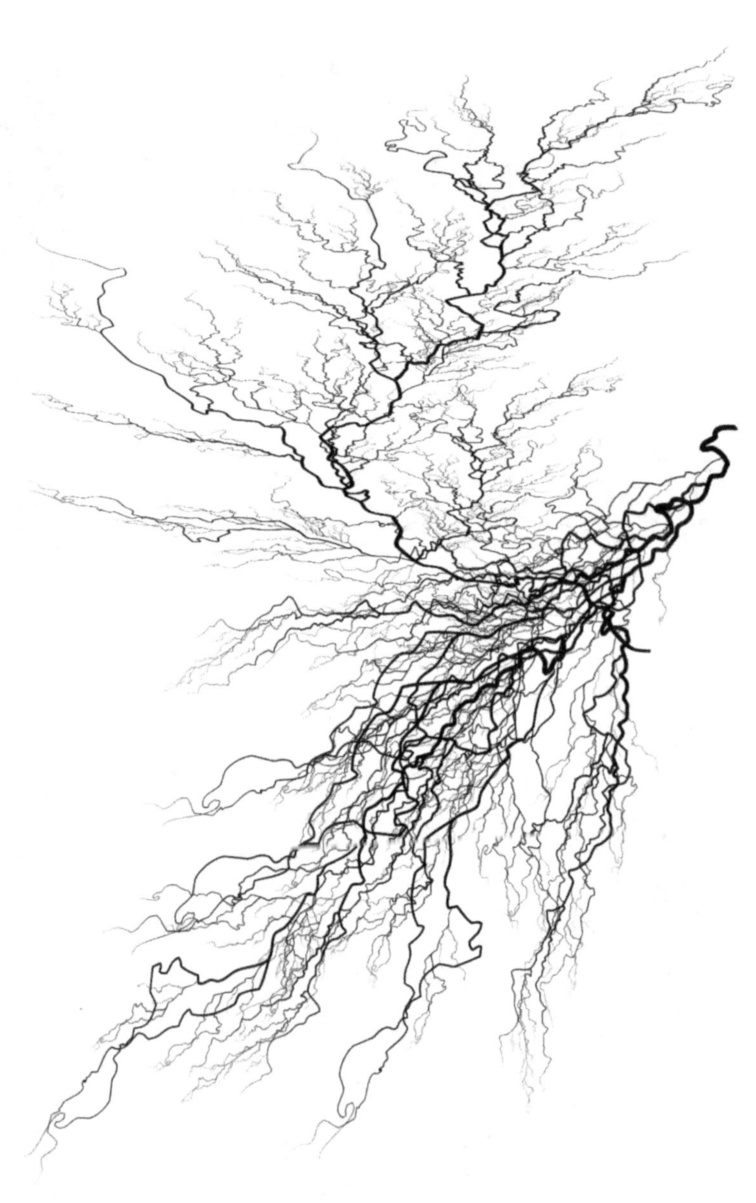

# 22. Helogale

The familiar notes floated through the mesh and danced overhead.

Glass doors she'd flung open on the way to passing out the night before would've been no use anyway due to all the bass shaking the ridge as the sun came up.

"We are all just prisoners here of our own device," he lilted hoarsely against the flesh he'd spent the twilight tenderizing with his tongue.

"The prison is a prism," Nyula muttered down at him from further away than she'd wanted to be.

Kusimanse wryly looked up at her bleary face then over towards the balcony and blushgrinned. "Your jailers are back~" he whispered.

The gang of levitating hummingbirds froze mid-air at being seen by him. Feeling her eyes slash towards them a few beats ahead of her actually doing it knocked them back a bit.

A giant crow dropped onto the balcony and goose-stepped towards the metallic screen with perverse authority, like it could see exactly the positions that they were in under the tangle of sheets and was not amused.

She deftly slid her hands into his monchichi hair and pulled him up to her chest before covering his eyes, knowing he wouldn't survive seeing the shapeshift.

"This can't be allowed to- he can't keep doing this-" Virac Ocha's vibrato shook her cell as humanoid appendages spun out proximally from his center like a warrior moving from dragon to eagle to crow.

"You can't stop him-" she grinned darkly.
"This was not part of the deal-" Virac Ocha fussed.

"He's the only reason I haven't said fuck your "deal," she countered abrasively, "and you can't stop him."

"Is he gone yet?"Kusi muttered up from his frequency.

"...no," she growled as the hummingbirds attending her cage crossed the threshold into her pen two at a time, shifting into human form all together.

"They always smell like copal," he sighed happily under the sheets and held her tighter as her pulse slowed down.

*

"Sr. VIRA," one of the most colorful ones present whispered. The muscles twitched in the side of Viracocha's face, letting Salyr know to continue.

"She looks much better fed by the bamboo than she did by the sand-"

Virac Ocha grunted." I'm not to care how she-"
"The inability of the outer cage to remain clean kept her from-" he said cloyingly.
"I have No interest in the cleanliness of cages-" Virac Ocha spat.
"Yessir, but she does...and try as it might, That beach was in a fight for its-" The one nicknamed Arete called out.

“Enough!-” Virac Ocha seethed. “She was writing!”

“Not like here, Virac.”

Virac Ocha’s attention danced over to the most laconic and somberly festooned one in her retinue.

Malak looked up, feeling the weight of the eyes of his technical superior with less field experience on him. “It’s the nature of it. Including however the fuck he…is doing that. Here too. Besides. I actually read it.”

Virac Ocha’s eyes rolled as Malak continued, nonplussed.

“Not only do I read ALL of it, you only outrank me and anyone currently attending her because we believe so much that we passed on promotions.” he hissed softly. ” Multiple. Promotions.”

Virac Ocha's eyes slid to the petty officers that surrounded him and realized they'd slit his throat. For her. And get away with it.

"It's okay," Malak stepped closer. "We let you forget that." Viracocha squared up to Malak's defiance of rank, ready for whatever came next.

"Don't let that be a mistake, Virac." Malak growled softly. "Survey... the actuality...of the situation versus...the goal...SIR."

At his heart as much as a "company man" one could be in the realm, Virac Ocha felt the weight of those who technically reported to him like the unspoken threat he'd always known the outfit to be, even before he'd been assigned to replace the last leader.

He shook his feathers out, agitated because he didn't know if any of the upper or adjacent guard would believe him or even care. He laughed, saving face. "You sure seem to have a lot of words for being known as the quiet one, " Viracocha chuckled stiffly.

"Only when necessary, " Malak grinned back. The smile didn't reach his eyes.

Virac Ocha turned on his heels and screeched maniacally down at Nyula. she winced, never releasing her protective grip around Kusi's eyes.

"Hold on a," she casually code-switched frequencies and glared balefully at the feathered one they all knew was a fucking snake to the core who'd just found out she was the mongoose.

"Yes?" she drawled, smirking. The smile didn't reach her eyes either.

"You will... meet this quota-" Virac Ocha squawked abusively in her face.

She wiped the thin spray of spittle off of her cheek, leaned in and growled. "When have I ever not?"

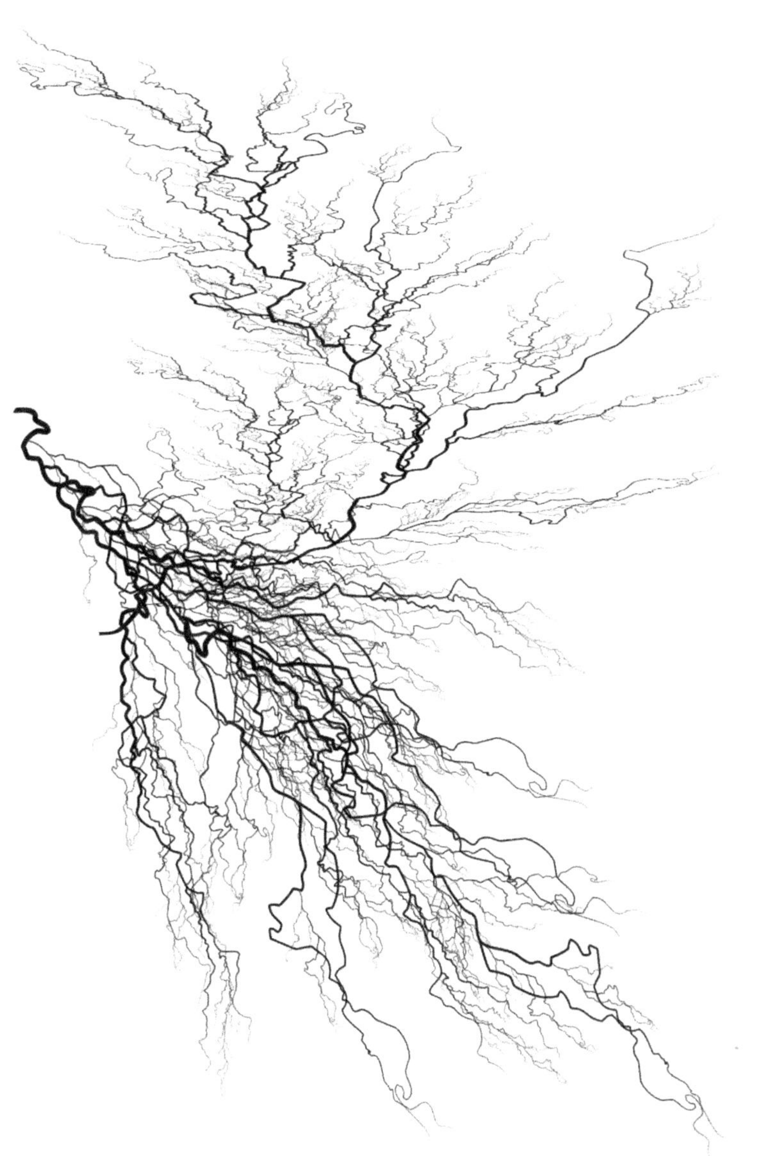

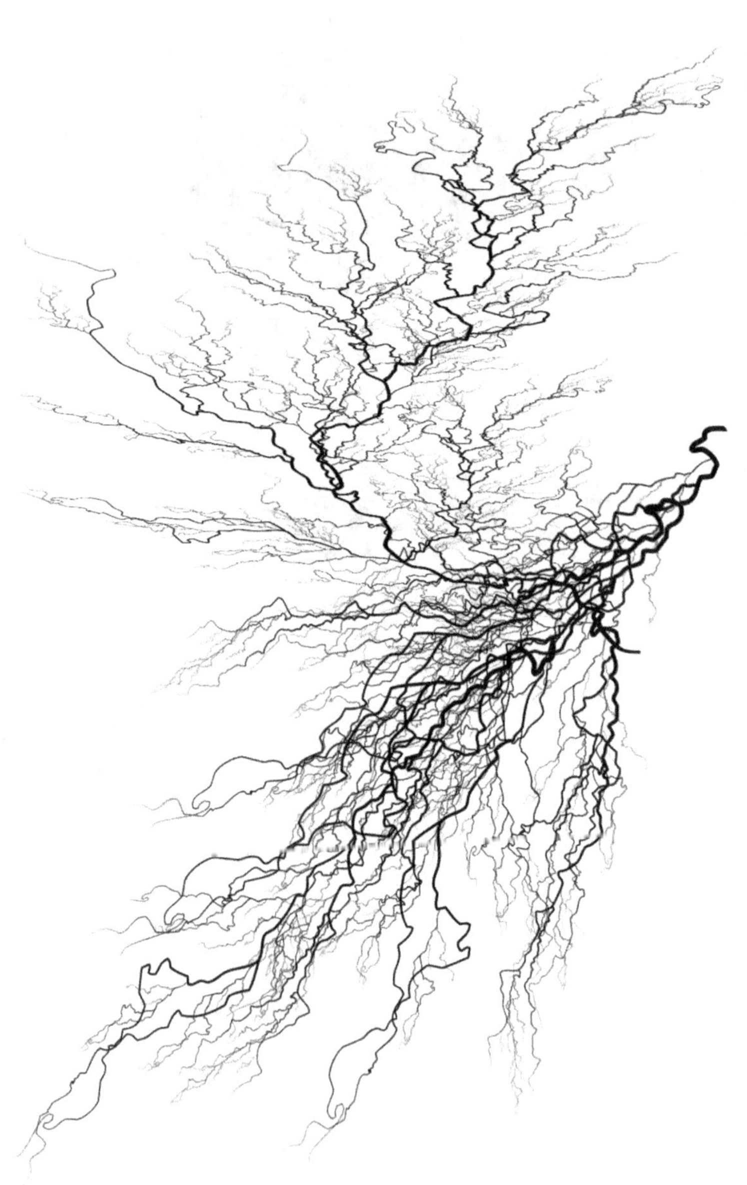

# 23. US.

She felt like nothing more than a tuft of hair over a pile of plaid after the episode.

"Yet still I rise," she muttered.

He reached in and dusted the crumbs from barbeque chips he'd never seen her eat until lately off her nose. She grunted in protest until he absently waved the rocks glass of shoddy rosé that actually paired nicely with the chips under her nose.

She sheepishly peeked out from under her protective mess of hair as both hands preemptively vice-gripped around his wrists to stop any attempt at playing airplane with the hooch.

Her neck craned out of her Stewart tartan shell as he leveraged the wine away from her lips all the same until she was almost off balance.

He darted in and kissed her cheek. "Enough already," he gently growled against her eye socket, "Fuck the DAY…we're gonna make tha Night good," he whispered as his mouth planted a scratchy kiss on her third eye. "Now write, you-"

She groaned as her third eye popped open and got the rest of her into gear.

She grabbed her writing phone with one hand, the drink with the other and swigged before bogarting a gruff kiss off of him, then threw a cold thigh across him into his always warm lap and instantly picked up the stands of the soliloquy that'd been tossed to the side the last time they'd disengaged from writerhead without missing a beat.

Time left them alone.

The silence of her fingers slipping across the screen and the soft scratch of his pen playing across paper were only interrupted by her third eye telepathically whispering thanks to his and the sound of her silky shorts drawing themselves across his bare skin when he'd pulled her hips more into his lap.

They crawled out of the string theory k-hole strung up between themselves to respectively re-up on booze or snacks, walking with whomever they each happened to be fleshing out in sessions like these.

Even though they existed in completely different universes that had nothing to do with each other, their respective entities hung out like demons drinking together at bars that the two humans they concerned themselves with couldn't see , only without the torment and enmity. When he'd realized that this was what her heart longed for with him it was one of the strangest moments of his life.

When he realized what this actually was had been one of the sweetest.

Time tapped back in to let them know it was almost up.

"Get anything good?" she asked, clocking the carac he was

creating as it marveled at what had become of its limbs in

this session.

"Turned out they're more sinewy than I thought," he

murmured, "which explained the tenacity-"

"Yeah, that motherfucker looks like he could survive an

explosion-" she whistled appreciatively. "All I got was Us,"

she blushed and looked away.

"Maybe it's about time for you to start to all the way see

it," he murmured. He grabbed her chin and turned her

back to him." Your eyes look better."

"Yeah?"

"Yeah."

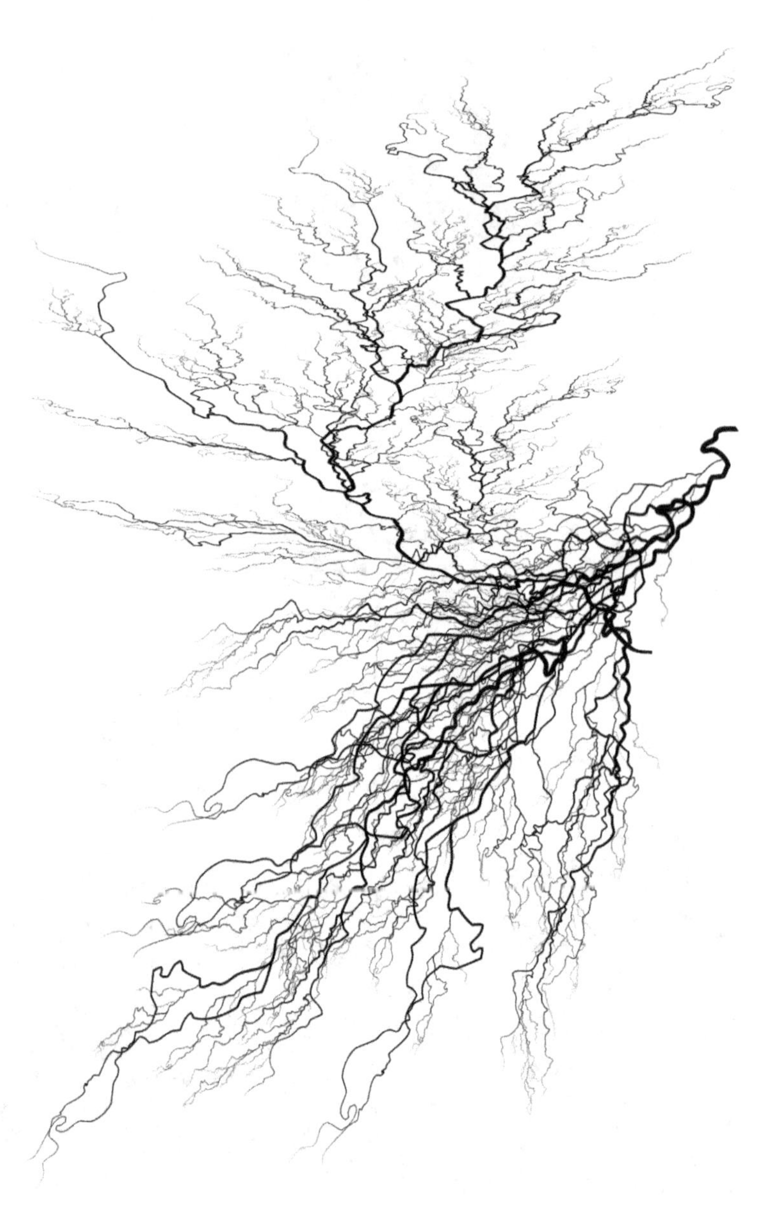

# 24. Haze

"Are you sure you want to do this? You know she wants to feed. " her guardian asked plainly.

"That's because she's only had milk..." the younger angel said with a strange look dancing just under the surface of her skin. Alarmed, he looked at her as she walked away.

"Oh my G- what are you planning on doing? " he yelled after her as she locked the big door between them.  When she turned around he was nose to nose with her all the same, the rest of her retinue surrounding them both.

He raised an eyebrow as his eyes whited out, making the crinkling of hallowed flesh around his sockets all the more obscene as he tried to hide his happiness. "You finally are ready, aren't you?"he muttered, the slash of his beatific mouth thick with dark joy.

"Just... have my back, " she sang out and skipped down the hill.

Her main guardian looked around at the others, stupefied.

"Burner mode?" Brilutus asked casually, enjoying Narok trying to contain his glee.

"Set to Char, maan! Just like that! Outta nowhere-"

"We sorta saw it coming, " Awkqiphan quipped.

"How?" Narok crowed.

"See! You're too close-" yelled Daijah.

"It's okay- we're here for the shore up, we got the periphery-"

"...but how did y'all even-" Narok asked his fellow brethren, mystified.

"Having to literally dry out after the hungry bunch was a big tell. Suit up?"

"Suit up, Fells, flying towards fire in the whole!"

*

By the time the fallen angels assigned to keep perim around the neophyte fought their way through the rampant principalities at play only a few beats above the heads of charges below the fire was already burning with the two of them smack dab in the middle of it.

They watched the feeder who'd misread the Bodhisattva energy of commission and compassion for those weaknesses that signaled a feeding frenzy to those being spiritually processed flinch in horror as the eyes of Phoenix devoured every lie offered for the unmitigated revelation of a truth that'd never be forgotten.

It was a bloodbath of the highest caliber, the feeder picked so clean by the heat of Phoenix's brimstone that it lay there, exhausted in broad daylight, each pupil splitting into two as it choked on the purifying meat already in its belly before choking on it had begun.

"...you okay?" Phoenix asked simply to the body housing the beauty and the beast before her. Their whimpers got tangled into one and were spat off their tongue like her query of concern was even more of a purgative.  "I give no fucks for shadows. Heal, love. Gotta go." Phoenix popped up like a kid and went to hug her friend goodbye.

"No!" the demon trying to string her out roared and pulled her friend's body out of the way as if Phoenix was brimstone itself.

She shrugged, chuckled and breezed through her gapemouthed arsenal on her way to an iced latte at her favorite joint.

"It's about got damn time! " Brilutus roared with pride.

Daijah chuckled, looking over at the heavenly hazed being processing ten times faster due to what she'd greedily inhaled. "About time indeed. "

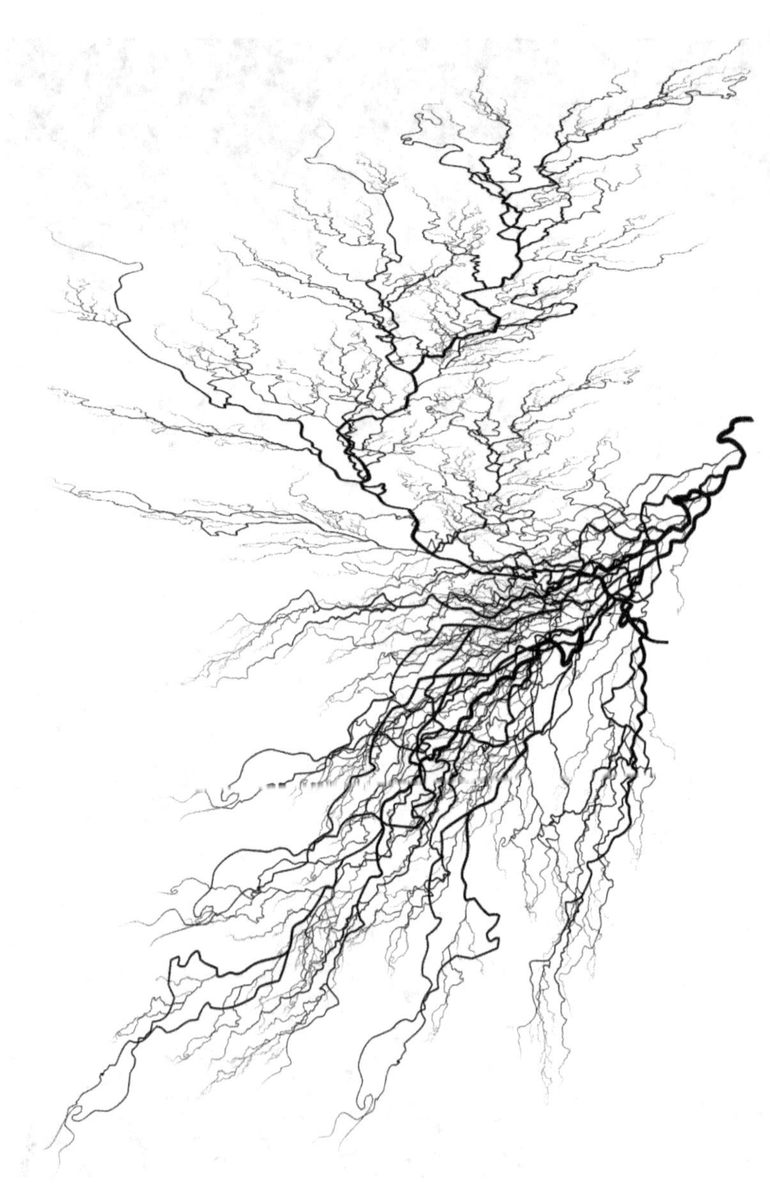

# 25. Trip

He'd watched her day after day walk around it as she drew. She didn't care that he saw her do it, that much he knew.The part of her that would've given a fuck had evaporated like it always did in times like these. He still felt like he was spying, even though he knew he was allowed. Because of the other one that rose up when this fell on her.  The part that suffered no fools, that would smite shit instead of opening things for discussion that flew in the face of what It had been awakened to do.

He was never sure if that aspect liked him as much as the rest or just was tolerating his presence. But he was sure it would pin him to the wall like it was an Arabian cave and choke the life force out of him just as readily as word had gotten around it had done to others before him at the slightest infraction.

There was alot of pacing.
Seen.
From his perch.

Her bony, attenuated feet wore dull grooves into the otherwise gleaming mahogany floors the dropcloths were spread over.

When she'd rest he'd be transfixed by how the arches of her usually almost flat feet seemed to pull higher up into her body day by day in mode, stunned by the actuality of the bubbling brooks in the pads of her feet being activated, softly hissing and spinning as she slept. She seemed stilled by the sound, only to wake up startled and start walking around in circles again between drawing jags, staring down into the wormhole.

Like she was waiting.
For something.

He fell asleep to the slap of her feet as she padded around as usual.

He woke to the sound of her gasp and looked over at her standing on the edge of her drawing with this bewildered grin on her face. His knuckles went white like his limbs understood before his head did as his highest self roughly snapped back online.

"Wait! DON'T! " he screamed as the love of his every life looked up at him like a simultaneously lucid and deranged five year old, down into the wormhole she'd drawn and jumped onto it like a child playing hopscotch as he flung himself off the bed after her, tackling her off of it in midair and onto the couch in a heap.

"What the fuck is wrong with you!?!"he roared as he pinned her down, "you promised! You fucking promised not to Do that any-"

She wrapped her arms around his panicked shoulders and kissed him gingerly on his third eye until he calmed down.

" I'm not- I'm not leaving- I'm not leaving again, I was only playing around-" she whispered, placating him.

“YOU...you...you have no idea what it was like! No idea how long it took me to find you last time!” he yelled angrily against her thymus chakra.

“Yes, I do...”she murmured, ” it was No time, remember?...cause there’s no-“

“You shut- you shut your face! You and your No time, you fucking bodhisattva! It was time! It Was tiiiime!”he screamed.

She wordlessly kissed him on the lips.
“SO HELP me God, if you Do it again-” he growled.

She kissed him again. “Woaw~God? You’re bringing up-” she chuckled.
“Anima, I will f ureaking kill you-“he snarled.

"I know, Animus-"she sighed and kissed him again. "... but it's certainly nice to have you awake here all the way with me again."she murmured against the shards of silver impacted down the sides of his chiseled, bronzed face as if by force.

He huffed petulantly and lifted her up to carry her back to bed, absently stepping onto the center of the drawing as he went.

"FUCK!" he screamed as the drawing activated, opening underneath the both of them.

"Just hold on this tiiime!"she yelled joyfully like the spiritual adrenaline junkie she was as they slammed through the vortex into nothing, disappearing into the floor as the ether was rocked by his terrified curses.

**The end. Of the beginnings.**

If you would've Told me when all this began that we were gonna Hafta do a part two...

fire
walker
c o v i d compendium
by Angel
Brynner

...Coming soon~

Angel Brynner

# cautantowwit

## (Indian Summer)

Part travelogue, part oral history and visual
Documentation of a honeymoon phase with a city like
No place else  on earth,  The Bottom of The Ninth Ward Bulletins
chronicle  American artist and author  Angel Brynner's
First sojourn in New Orleans.

Originally sent out from her blog The Art of Life while she was
Volunteering with re-builders and missionaries alongside
The American Peace Corps in New Orleans as the city continued
its recovery effort, BNWB documents  all she was allowed to witness
For whosoever was  tuning in beyond  friends and family across the globe.

These are the tales of the survivors, those who refused to be washed away by
The neglect of a country they were born  and raised in...

This edition also features artwork from the NYC2NOLA series of collages  from the
Angel Brynner/Art of Life project, a ten+ year trek through creative
Communities across America, Canada, Mexico & the Caribbean that
produced over 1500 pieces of work on the road.style.

# BOTTOM OF THE NINTH WARD

**TENTH ANNIVERSARY EDITION**

**Blackwater Rising picks up where
Bottom of the Ninth Ward Bulletins left off**

**Blackwater Rising is what rises up when you
Trouble the water so as to be healed..**

# Coming soon from 

## B LACK WA TER R ISING

by Angel Brynner

## ABOUT THE AUTHOR

Author and multimedia artist Angel Brynner has marched to the beat of her
own drum across the arts for over two decades. After formal training with
the vanguard of the menswear industry she helmed her own line of men's
clothing and produced events for the collection in the club scenes of
New York and Tokyo.

She became quietly known for the futuristic cautionary tales back-dropping
her collections, taking over clubs and the guerilla-marketing style she used
to slam her vision into the hearts of her fans. While being sponsored by
Multinational companies desiring audience with her underground tribe, she
returned from Japan to her hometown to press charges against a pedophile
before the statute of limitations ran out.

Cast as a vigilante by a corrupt sex crimes unit for trying to protect another
child from the same attacker, during the media onslaught against
the first brave adults to come forward and press charges against
the Catholic priests that had abused them as children she was hit with a
vision of all those already lost in a sick war on kids no one talked about.

She committed herself & her art to doing something about it.

The grievechronic universe was forged in the fires of imagining the
Armageddon that would erupt through a generation of kids who
had finally had enough abuse at the hands of adults and
banded together under their grievances.
The epic spiritual, metaphysical, and historical implications
of such an event played out on every level- from the hellish norms
that caused it to what would be called heaven by such a broken world-
made her head spin.

Published by Kokopellima Press, each  free-standing installment of grievechronic
Is a  take-no- prisoners tale.

Alongside AOLAB[the active-art series featuring the multimedia work
that fed Eutaxis, Ecclesia, Exodus, Erebus, Exist and the kinetic collection
of novels that follow them]. Angel Brynner's books are the culmination of
an artistic journey many years in the making.
all leading to a mysterious future project entitled **Transcendence.**

# ...Want more?

Email info@kokopellimapress.com

For access to exclusive, free and special edition goods tied to all things Angel Brynner / AOLAB \ Globalboho.

...and check out www.grievechronic.com

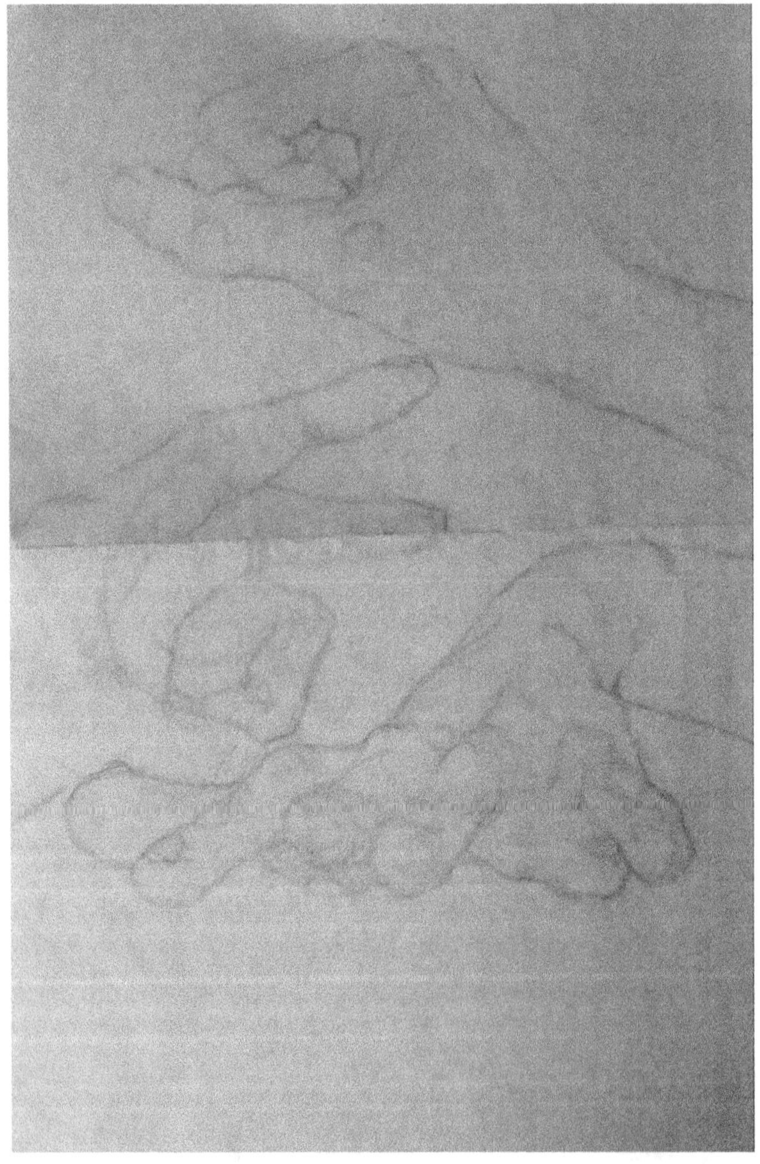

KOKOPELLIMA PRESS

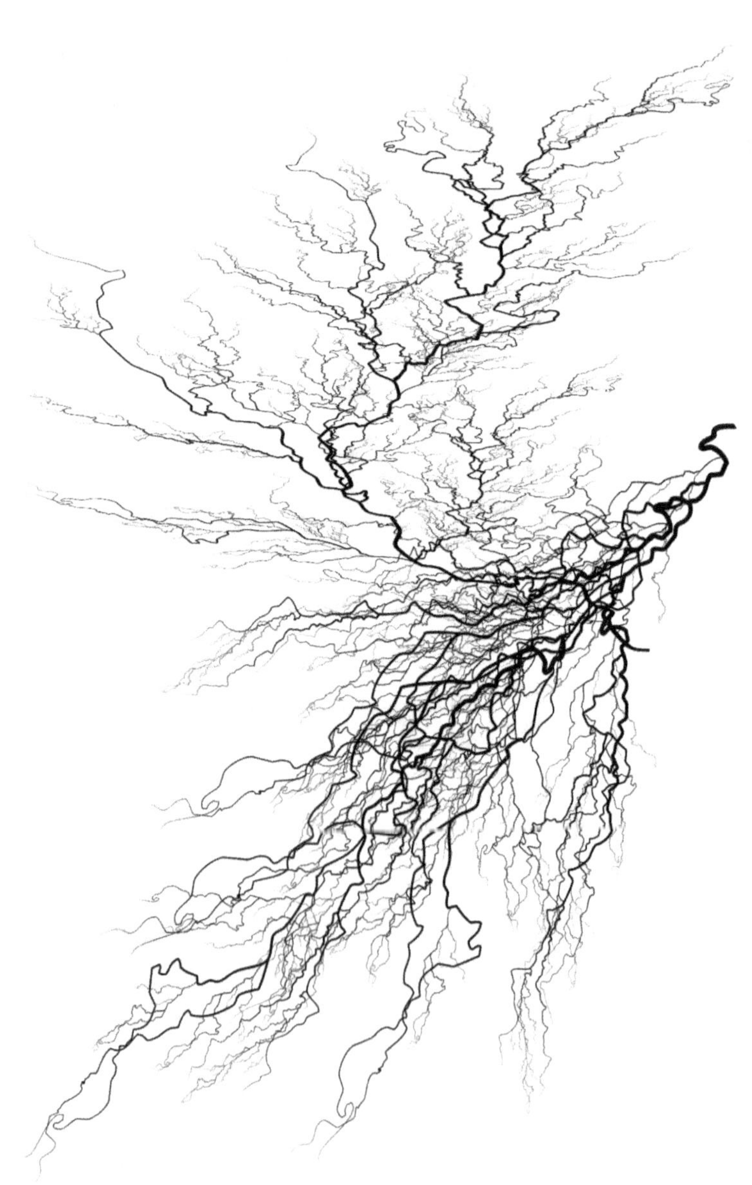